DAWN OF LOVE

Bitter Creek left Rose's bed at the first crack of dawn. It was raining. Rose could hear the water hitting the windows and dripping down, and the creaking of the bare tree branches in the stiff winter winds.

"Where are you going, darling?" she asked, watching Bitter Creek dress hurriedly.

"My beautiful Rose," he whispered. "It will take that posse quite a while to get here, especially through this rain, but the sooner I leave the safer it is for you."

"But, our time together was too short—" Rose's words caught in her throat, choked by emotion. Her green eyes glowed with tears that reflected the dawn's light.

"Rose," Bitter Creek murmured, leaning down with a kiss for her. "I'll be back soon."

And, with that, he was gone. . . .

LEATHER AND LACE

#1: THE LAVENDER BLOSSOM   (1029, $2.50)
by Dorothy Dixon
Lavender Younger galloped across the Wild West under the black banner of Quantrill. And as the outlaw beauty robbed men of their riches, she robbed them of their hearts!

#2: THE TREMBLING HEART   (1035, $2.50)
by Dorothy Dixon
Wherever Jesse James rode, Zerelda rode at his side. And from the sleet of winter to the radiance of fall, she nursed his wounds—and risked her life to be loved by the most reckless outlaw of the west!

#3: THE BELLE OF THE RIO GRANDE   (1059, $2.50)
by Dorothy Dixon
Belle Star blazed her way through the wild frontier with two ambitions: to win the heart of handsome Cole Younger, the only man who could satisfy her fiery passion—and to be known as the west's most luscious outlaw!

#4: FLAME OF THE WEST   (1091, $2.50)
by Dorothy Dixon
She was the toast of the New York stage, a spy during the Civil War, and the belle of the Barbary Coast. And her passionate untamed spirit made her the unforgettable legend known as the FLAME OF THE WEST!

#5: CIMARRON ROSE   (1106, $2.50)
by Dorothy Dixon
Cimarron Rose lost her heart on sight to the notoriously handsome outlaw "Bitter Creek" Newcombe. She rode with the infamous Billie Doolin gang, and if she had to lie, steal, cheat or kill, she would—to keep the only man she ever really loved!

#6: HONEYSUCKLE LOVE   (1125, $2.50)
by Carolyn T. Armstrong
When Honeysuckle and Buck met, desire spread like wildfire. She left her home and family to ride the countryside—and risk her life—for the rapture of love!

#7: DIAMOND QUEEN   (1138, $2.50)
by Dorothy Dixon
Alice was a seductive beauty whose gambler's intuition made her a frontier legend. And for Alice, the most arousing game of all was life—where the stakes were high and the winner took all!

Available wherever paperbacks are sold, or order direct from the Publisher. Send cover price plus 50¢ per copy for mailing and handling to Zebra Books, 475 Park Avenue South, New Y N.Y. 10016. DO NOT SEND CASH.

#5
LEATHER AND LACE

CIMARRON ROSE

BY DOROTHY DIXON

ZEBRA BOOKS
KENSINGTON PUBLISHING CORP.

ZEBRA BOOKS

are published by

KENSINGTON PUBLISHING CORP.
475 Park Avenue South
New York, N.Y. 10016

Printed in the United States of America

To

Alice

Chapter 1

Beautiful Rose Dunn pushed back the cluster of rich brown curls from her forehead and tucked two daisies into her ringlets.

"Oh, Rose, you are always so smart," her sister, Ellie, cried in admiration. "Who else would think of putting daisies on her box for the box social and then putting daisies in her hair to match?"

"Yeah, Rose is the smart one," sneered Bree, their older brother. "She's the one that got to go to Kansas City to get more schoolin'."

"And you've been jealous of her ever since," Rebecca Dunn accused.

"Well, she's Pa's favorite," Bree said angrily.

"As if Pa had a favorite!" Rose said crisply. "I think he hates us all."

"Everyone will know that the box with the daisies is yours," Rebecca said. "I wish a certain person would know which box is mine."

"I guess you mean Bill Eckridge," Daniel, their younger brother, put in. "Why don't you put roses on your box and a rose in your hair?"

"Bill Eckridge doesn't know I'm alive," Rebecca said mournfully. "He always bids on Rose's box."

The three Dunn sisters, Rose, Rebecca, and

Ellie, were at the kitchen table. Each had a box before her. Their two brothers, Bree and Daniel, were interested watchers.

Ma Dunn was frying chicken at the black iron stove. She was a thin woman with sallow skin, her hair was pulled straight back from her hawkish face. Under her soiled apron, there was a revealing lump. She was about four months pregnant.

Rose looked with pity at Ma and offered again to fry the chicken.

Ma grunted, "I kin do it."

Rose sighed, remembering the conversation she and Rebecca had had the night before, Rebecca had asked if Rose didn't think that Ma was too old to have a baby.

"It's not that she's so old," Rose had answered. "It's just that she's all dried up. The last four babies have been born dead."

"Poor Ma."

"I often wonder if Ma was ever young and pretty. I wonder if she ever liked to laugh," Rose said softly.

"No, I think Ma was born old. I remember when Pa brought her here after our mamma died. I remember thinking that she was a little old woman," Rebecca reminisced.

"Oh, Rebecca, you can't remember that far back!"

"Yes, I can. I remember we were all gathered in the kitchen waiting to see our new mamma. Pa brought Ma in. She stared at us and we stared at her, and she didn't smile and neither did any of us."

"Rebecca, wouldn't you hate to be married to Pa?" Rose asked.

Rebecca shuddered. "I can't imagine anything worse than having to go to bed with Pa. He smells terrible. I've listened to him rooting around like a pig night after night all my life."

"I remember when I was about seven or eight and you and I were sleeping on the trundle bed," Rose murmured. "I woke up and I heard Pa rootin' and takin' on like he does. He was mad at our mamma and he was cussing her while he was boring into her. I yelled, 'Leave Mamma alone. Leave my mamma alone. You're always hurting her.' And Pa reached down and hit me in the mouth. I felt the blood pouring out, and I started to wail when he hit me again."

"And then?" Rebecca asked breathlessly. "What happened then?"

"I shut up. I thought he would kill me."

"You never told me about this before."

"Because from that moment I hated him and when Mamma died I believed he killed her. And I hated him even more," Rose declared savagely.

Rose was jolted back to the present when Ma set a platter of fried chicken on the table.

"Why do girls always bring fried chicken in their boxes?" Daniel asked.

"Because men like fried chicken," Ellie, the oldest of the Dunn sisters, said demurely.

The girls began to fill their boxes with the chicken and with light bread which Ma had placed on the table, too.

Rose carefully tied the lid on her box and then

tucked in the cluster of daisies and trailing ivy.

Daniel went out to the lane adjoining the farmhouse and returned with a bouquet of wild pink roses.

"Fix up your box, Rebecca. If Bill doesn't bid high enough on Rose's box, he might bid on yours," he said encouragingly.

Rebecca began to decorate her box enthusiastically.

"There's some nice clover out in back," Daniel said now to Ellie. "It would make a real nice decoration for your box."

"No, thanks," Ellie said. "Buck says it's foolish to decorate a box for a box special."

"Ellie Dunn!" Rose exploded. "You aren't going to listen to anything that horrible Buck Ansel says?"

Ellie ducked her blond head shyly and blushed.

"He's a mean man," Rose declared vehemently. "He's already killed two wives."

"Don't say that," Ellie said sharply and all the Dunns looked at her. Ellie was always so quiet and so gentle.

"He's a mean cuss," Bree put in definitely. "Aunt Celestine Riggs, who always dresses the dead, said both his wives had welts on them from being beaten by a strap."

There was dead silence now.

Ma sighed heavily.

"You stay away from Buck Ansel," Daniel said darkly. "There's some men that are just mean down to their soul. Buck's one of them and so is Pa."

Six pairs of eyes looked around fearfully. It

seemed that the menacing presence of Pa was always with them.

"It's that damned strop," Daniel mumbled. "Pa keeps that damned strop hanging there where it's handy."

"He's stropped us plenty," Bree rasped. "Those splotches of blood on that strop are from you and me, Daniel."

"The time is coming," Daniel predicted, "when we can strop him."

Ma looked around fearfully. "Hush, boys, hush," she whispered.

Chapter 2

When the Dunns arrived at the church box social in their old buckboard, everyone was delighted to see them.

Bill Eckridge rushed to the wagon to assist Rose in alighting. At the sight of him, Rebecca's heart was in her eyes; they sparkled with love for him.

Everyone trailed after Rose, Rebecca, and Ellie as they took their boxes to the long table under the giant oak three in the side yard. There Rev. Timothy Falters would auction them off.

Rose, surrounded by young men each threatening to outbid the others for the pleasure of eating with her, was dimpling and laughing.

And then she noticed the stranger!

He was dressed in white buckskin. He wore a huge sombrero with a red, white, and blue band around it. His hair, peeping from under that huge hat, was the color of dark rich honey. His eyes were the color of Oklahoma blue skies, and were strikingly set off by tawny gold skin and lashes as black as the wing of a blackbird.

He was staring at her in open admiration.

The bidding for the boxes began.

Rev. Falters held up Ellie's box.

Buck Ansel yelled, "Fifty cents."

Ellie lowered her eyes and flushed deep apricot.

Rose's heart ached for Ellie. Fifty cents indeed! Buck could have at least bid a dollar which was the amount for which most of the boxes were sold. But his bid took the box.

Now the minister was holding up a daisy-starred box.

"It's yours, Rose," Rebecca whispered.

Bill Eckridge led off with a dollar bid.

"One dollar and a half," shouted Henry Andrews.

"One dollar and sixty cents," someone else chimed in.

"One dollar and eighty cents," another bid.

"Two dollars," Bill Eckridge cried.

Then a clear cool voice trilled above all the rest: "Five dollars."

There was absolute silence.

No box had ever brought five dollars!

The stranger went forward, paid the five dollars, and accepted the proffered box as Rose went forward to claim the box as hers.

The bidding proceeded quickly now. Rose was delighted to see Bill Eckridge had bid a dollar for Rebecca's box, but she watched uncomfortably as Ellie nervously opened her plain box and Buck grabbed the largest piece of chicken.

Rose and the stranger, who had introduced himself as George Newcomb, found a place under a tree, and she opened the box as he grinned at her.

"Fried chicken?" he teased.

She smiled and asked, "How did you know there would be fried chicken in my box?"

"Church-box-social boxes always have fried chicken," he declared.

"And have you been to many church box socials?" she questioned dimpling.

"Yes." He smiled displaying teeth as white as curd.

"You are a very handsome man, George Newcomb," she stated.

"And you are a beautiful woman," he said simply. "So beautiful that when I first saw you I thought I was seeing things."

"Thank you, sir."

They ate in silence.

Suddenly they heard the sound of a hard slap and looked to see Link, Buck's eight-year-old son, falling backward off the bench.

Ellie half-rose to help the lad.

"Leave him be," Buck rasped.

"He only reached for another piece of chicken," Ellie protested. "I put in extra for the boys."

Buck glared at Ellie and stared menacingly at Link.

There was a bright red stain across the boy's cheek, but, despite the tears in his eyes, he did not whimper as he picked himself up.

"He asks me first and he knows it," Buck growled. "He'll get a good one when he gets home."

"For shame!" Ellie cried.

"There, there, don't fret yourself," Buck drawled to Ellie. "I know how to handle my boys.

They know what they're goin' to get if they do wrong."

"The brute!" Rose said to George. "What those poor little boys need is love, not beatings."

"The man is a coward," George said definitely. "Men like him take out their hates on the helpless."

"I'd like to give him a good beating," Rose declared hotly.

"He'll get what's coming to him someday," George said.

"I hope so, but, George, my sister can't stand up to his meanness. You heard her now. She's scared of him. Everybody's scared of him. No one dared bid more than his fifty cents for Ellie's box."

"I saw the heartbreak on your face when Ellie was humiliated by that cheap bid," George said.

"I'm so afraid he'll ask her to marry him. She feels so sorry for those two boys," she said sadly.

"Can't your pa talk to her?"

"Pa? He's as mean as Buck Ansel."

"We'll have to figure something out to keep Ellie away from Buck," he said definitely.

"We?" she questioned.

"We," he repeated. "I intend to see more of you, Rose Dunn."

"I would like that," she said frankly.

"You are beautiful and sweet and kind. I saw, too, how happy you were when your admirer, Bill, selected your sister's box when he couldn't have yours."

"Rebecca has liked Bill Eckridge for a long time," Rose explained.

"I could see how happy she was when he bid on her box."

"You really notice everything," Rose said admiringly.

"In my line of work you have to notice everything," he said dryly.

"What kind of work do you do?" she asked.

"Someday I will tell you," he promised, smiling. "Now tell me about yourself. I know you are very beautiful and that you are kindhearted and that you have two sisters, Ellie and Rebecca, and that your pa is mean like Buck."

"I have two brothers. Bree is twenty years old and he looks and acts like my pa. Daniel is seventeen and is very quiet and . . . and sweet. I have a stepmother," she said and stopped talking to look at him.

"Do you love your stepmother?"

"Why do you ask?"

"Because you looked troubled when you mentioned her," he explained.

"Oh, George, she's such a poor thing. She has one baby after another and all of them born dead. And she gets scrawnier and weaker every time. She's been married to Pa for seven years."

"That's too bad," he said sympathetically. "And how old were you when your real ma died?"

"I was nine years old, Ellie was eleven, and Rebecca, seven. I always felt that Pa killed mamma," she cried.

"But why would you feel that way?"

"Because she was always having babies, too, and just got plump wore out," she murmured.

He was silent as he helped himself to another piece of chicken.

"Rose, you must have a very low opinion of marriage," he said presently, softly.

"When I hear the word 'marriage,'" she answered, "it makes me sick."

"Someday," he whispered, "I will make you change your opinion of marriage."

"I doubt if anyone could ever make me change my opinion of marriage, George. I'll always remember Pa and my two mammas."

When the social was over, he escorted her to the buckboard.

As they waited for the others, he told her, "I will be back in two or three weeks, Rose. I am going to follow your buckboard now so I will know where you live."

"You will have to watch out for Pa," she said. "I told you he was mean."

"And you are only sixteen years old," he stated simply.

She was amazed. "How did you know that? I didn't tell you my age."

"You said you were nine years old when your own ma died and you and your other ma have been related for seven years," he explained and added, "I'm sure your pa married your stepmother soon after your mamma died."

"Yes, he used the excuse that we young ones needed a mamma," she said dryly.

"So you're sixteen and Ellie is eighteen and Rebecca is fourteen and if we're to keep Ellie from making a terrible mistake, we'll have to work fast."

"We just can't let her marry that awful Buck Ansel," Rose cried.

"We won't," he whispered as the others approached the wagon. "I wish I could kiss you goodby, my beautiful Rose."

She smiled at him and wondered if she really would see him again.

Chapter 3

A late-spring rain was falling when Rose and Rebecca did their morning chores. Yellow-hearted peach blossoms, freed by the soft rain, sailed across the lowering sky like butterflies. As they milked the cows along with Bree and Daniel, they chattered of the events of the day before.

"You should have gone with us, Bree," Rose told the sullen-faced Bree as she watched the warm sweet milk flow like liquid gold into the bucket.

"Church box socials are a waste of time," he snarled.

"Wish I could have gone," Daniel put in. "I would have gone if I'd had any money to bid on a box."

"Well, Pa ain't about to give you any money until you're eighteen," Bree pointed out. "And then he won't give you much. I ought to know."

"Well, when I'm eighteen I'm going to get a little money together and take off."

"Where you intendin' to go?" Bree asked, interested.

"Guess there's not many more gold strikes being made, but I can always get a job as cowpuncher or a farm hand where I'd get paid a wage."

"Well, I'm stayin' right here. I want this farm someday," Bree said.

"You can have my share of the farm," Daniel said.

"And mine," Rose cried. "I don't want to stay here forever either."

"I don't want any part of the farm either," Rebecca put in now. "There're only sad memories here."

"Anyway, we had a happy time yesterday didn't we?" Rose smiled.

"You once laughed about a knight on a white charger riding in from the west, Bree," Rebecca said, giggling. "But it really and truly happened. A handsome stranger rode in and he fell in love with our Rose."

"You ate with a stranger?" Bree barked.

"He was a gentleman," Rose said firmly.

"And he bid five dollars for her box," Rebecca said proudly.

"He must be a robber," Bree said darkly. "Nobody's got five dollars to bid on a box at a box social."

"Well, he did bid five dollars, and because he did, Bill bid on my box and I got to eat with Bill and that was wonderful!" rejoiced Rebecca.

The milking finished, Bree and Daniel went off to carry the filled buckets to the milk house while Rebecca and Rose went to gather eggs.

This was the only happy time in the girls' day; they could be together and talk.

They gathered the eggs now, holding to their soft young cheeks the warm ivory shells; some still had fluffy feathers clinging to them. When their baskets were full, they went to stand at the open barn entrance to wait for the rain to let up.

The sweet, clean fragrant odor of hay enveloped them as the soft pitter-patter of the raindrops on the barn roof tapered off.

"Rebecca, when we were in bed last night, Ellie whispered to me that Buck Ansel has asked to marry her."

Rebecca was shocked. "Oh, no, Rose. She wouldn't marry him!"

"He asked her yesterday at the box social," Rose said crisply, almost angrily. "And I thought everything was so perfect yesterday. The weather was so lovely and everybody was so happy except for Buck's hitting his poor little boy."

"I know," Rebecca said softly and began to cry.

"Don't cry, honey," Rose said. "Tears won't help. We've got to do something to keep her from marrying that mean man."

"She knows how terrible it is to live in the same house with someone like Pa, and Buck is even meaner," Rebecca said softly, looking around quickly to be sure that Pa wasn't within hearing distance.

Rose spoke solemnly now. "Rebecca, I'm going to tell you something I've never told to a living soul."

Rebecca looked askance at her sister.

"Promise me you'll never tell anyone," Rose urged. "Cross your heart and hope to die if you tell."

"I'll never, never tell," Rebecca vowed.

"Pa came at me one day in the barn. I had just finished gathering the eggs and I was alone. He sneaked up behind me, but I heard his footsteps and I whirled around and looked straight into his face."

"Oh, Rose, what did you do?" asked Rebecca breathlessly.

"It was awful. Pa's face was all screwed up ugly-like and his eyes had a strange look in them. He pushed his whiskers close to my face."

"How awful for you, my poor Rose."

"He was murmuring, 'Rose, Rose,' and he tried to run his hand up my dress. I tried to get away from him. He jerked me closer and felt my breasts."

Rebecca was speechless with horror now, but Rose continued her story.

"And then I told him I would scream and that seemed to bring him to his senses. He shoved me away and the next day he said he was sending me to school in Kansas City."

"Bree has always been so jealous because you got to go to school. If he only knew why!"

The rain had stopped now and the girls started for the farmhouse.

"I'll talk to Ellie tonight," Rose said quietly. "It would be a hell on earth to live with someone like Buck or Pa."

She cornered Ellie that evening when the dishes were done and Ma had collapsed weakly into bed.

"Let's walk down the lane, Ellie," Rose invited. "It's kind of cool. It gets cool when the sun goes down," Ellie protested.

"It's a beautiful evening. There's a full moon," Rose declared. "Here's your shawl."

When they were out of the farmhouse, Rose said, "Pa will be on her the minute we're gone."

"What do you mean?"

"Wake up, Ellie," Rose cried almost angrily. "You and I both know Pa is an animal. He jumps on poor old Ma every chance he gets. No wonder her babies are all born dead."

"You make it sound so awful."

"Some men are mean and selfish and that's the way Pa and Buck are and you can't be serious about thinking of marrying up with him!"

"I'd like a home of my own and I love those boys, Link and Hank."

"Do what you can for the boys, Ellie, but don't marry up with Buck. You heard how Aunt Celestine said his two dead wives had welts on their bodies when she prepared them for burial?"

"Maybe she just made that up," Ellie faltered.

"I'd believe it if Aunt Celestine said it was so," Rose said firmly.

"I'd like a baby," Ellie said weakly.

"Fine," Rose applauded. "Fine, but get a real man for your baby's father. Look at those poor cowed sons of his. Would you like a child of yours to look like that?"

Ellie said nothing.

"You're only eighteen years old," Rose reminded her. "You're not an old maid and you'll never be an old maid. You'll meet someone like our brother Daniel, someone kind."

Ellie still said nothing and presently went silently to bed.

Rose wondered if her words had made any impression on Ellie. She hoped so.

The next evening, Buck Ansel came to call on Ellie. They walked up the lane together as she and Ellie had done the evening before. But this time, when the walk up the lane was over and Ellie came into the farmhouse, there were stars in her eyes. Rose knew that Ellie had made a decision.

"Buck doesn't want a wedding party," Ellie told Rose later. "He thinks it's all foolishness."

"He's crazy," Rose cried. "Until you're Mrs. Buck Ansel you're still my sister and we're going to give you a proper wedding."

"Buck will be awful mad," Ellie protested.

"Let him be mad. He acts like he's always mad about something anyway. Have you ever seen him smile, Ellie?"

"Maybe . . . maybe I can make him happy," Ellie faltered.

"Men like Buck are never happy and seem to take pleasure in making everyone else unhappy," Rose blurted, "Oh, Ellie, please, please don't marry him."

"I promised," Ellie said quietly.

Rev. Timothy Falter came and friends of the Dunns came. Apparently Buck had no friends.

Rose thought Buck looked terrible. "He needs a good bath," she told Rebecca. "And look at the mud caked on his boots!"

The ceremony was to be held in the yard under a towering elm tree. It was a lovely day; the sun was shining and the birds were singing joyously. Daniel had gathered a huge mass of daisies and wild roses for the bride's bouquet and Rose had tucked a few of the flowers in Ellie's blond hair.

Ellie looked beautiful in her white Sunday-go-to-meeting dress. Her violet eyes glowed like amethysts.

"You look beautiful," Rose cried in admiration, looking at Ellie.

The sisters hugged each other and then Rose pulled away to say, "Ellie, promise me if you ever need me you'll let me know."

"I promise," Ellie whispered. "I promise."

"Do you, Buck Ansel, promise to take this woman, Ellie Dunn, as your lawfully wedded wife?"

Rose shut her mind against the words. But looking at Ellie and Buck, side by side, she thought: the Beauty and the Beast. It wasn't fair that Ellie's delicate loveliness should be given to the keeping of a brute like Buck. She saw Aunt Celestine Riggs hovering like the angel of death in the background. She could imagine what Aunt Celestine was thinking.

After the ceremony, food was set out on tables under the old trees. Daniel had gathered pink mallows to decorate the tables. While the wedding guests were eating and socializing, Rose generously offered to keep Link and Hank for a few days so

Ellie and Buck could enjoy some time alone for a honeymoon.

"Honeymoon, hell!" the man snorted. "Who needs a honeymoon? There's work to be done."

The newlyweds and the boys left early and after that the party became happier. There was group singing and Grandpa Ezra Riggs produced his fiddle and there was square-dancing.

Even poor old Ma with her misshapen belly seemed to enjoy the laughter and kept time to the music.

"I'll bet you wish your good-looking friend, George, was here" Rebecca whispered to Rose.

"He said he'd be back."

"Oh, Rose," Rebecca whispered. "Wouldn't it be wonderful if George came back and you fell in love with him and Bill liked me?"

Rose nodded. "It could happen, you know," she said happily.

Presently Rebecca confided, "You know, Rose, I keep thinking about poor Link and Hank. Did you notice how they cringed every time Buck looked at them?"

"How they must hate him! Just like we hate our pa."

"I thought Pa was going to strop Daniel until he was dead the other night," Rebecca said sadly. "Poor Daniel. He could hardly walk the next day."

"But he had to do his chores anyway." Rose added.

"Sometimes I think Pa is daft."

"He's just mean—but not as mean as Buck," Rose said darkly. "Look at Ma. She's actually smiling."

"Poor Ma," Rebecca sighed. "Poor all of us."

Chapter 4

Two days later, Ma went into labor and died.

"She was just plain tuckered out." Daniel wept.

Rose tried to comfort him. He was always so soft-hearted, so kind and loving. And he had tried to help Ma in every way he could.

"She's at rest, Daniel," Rose comforted. "She was so worn out. She just gave up."

Daniel went off then to fetch Aunt Celestine and Rose saddled old Nellie to ride to the neighboring farmhouses to spread the word of Ma's death.

She stopped first at Buck and Ellie's.

Buck greeted her at the door with, "What the hell do you want?"

Taken aback for a moment she could only stare at him.

Then Ellie came to the door and Rose was shocked to see that her eyes were swollen from crying and there was a big bruise on the side of her face.

The boys had followed her and their faces were splotched with tears.

Rose ignored the man and spoke to Ellie. "Ma's dead," she said simply. "She went into labor and was so weak she just died."

Ellis began to cry.

"Shut up your sniveling," the man rasped.

"Aunt Celestine is coming to dress Ma and we'll have the wake tonight and bury Ma tomorrow," Rose went on.

"And the baby?" Ellie asked softly.

"It's in Ma. They're both at rest."

"Ain't sure if we'll be there or not," Buck put in now.

Rose looked her amazement.

"Not be there," she echoed. "Of course, you'll be there. Ma is Ellie's mamma."

"Stepma," he sneered.

"Well, she was like our own ma to us. She did the best she could for us," Rose cried. "I have to get back. I'll see you at the wake."

"Good-by, Rose," Ellie said. "Thanks for coming to tell us."

On the way back home, Rose wondered what the future would hold for them.

She thought suddenly of those days she had spent at convent school in Kansas City. She was homesick for the convent garden and the scent of cut grass on the sooty strip of lawn. She longed to see the clean shadows of the huge trees etched by moonshine on the square blocks of the convent walls.

She thought of Sister Theresa with her incessant frown, her soft brown eyes, and loving hands. Sister Theresa had told her in parting, "I expect great things of you, dear Rose. God has given you great beauty and you have a most unusual character. You must make your own happiness."

She wished she could see Sister Theresa now and pour out her sorrow at Ma's passing. She slowed Nellie to a walk and found comfort in thinking of the May trees, in pink-and-white bloom, at the edge of the rather isolated convent garden. She thought of the shining long halls, the spotless windows with their prim touches of white. She remembered with longing the soft voices, the noiseless feet. And she remembered the sound of the organ and the scent of incense.

She lived again her sense of shock at coming home again to the old farmhouse and seeing Ma, always with child; and Pa, mean and domineering as ever; and Bree, glowering and jealous of her. Of course, the best part of her return was being with Ellie and Rebecca and Daniel again.

When she turned in at the Dunn lane she saw neighbors were already gathering, bringing food for the wake; soon she was enveloped by friendly sympathetic voices.

She made her way into a side room where she found Aunt Celestine dressing Ma in her best dress of dark blue.

"This was the only dress I could find that was decent enough for a laying-out," she greeted Rose. "Rebecca said this was her best one. Poor woman sure didn't have many clothes."

"No, Aunt Celestine, Ma didn't have much of anything. Just hard work and trying to have babies," Rose said sadly.

Aunt Celestine lowered her voice to a whisper. "I told her she should quit trying to have babies.

When she got in the family way I told her to take a good dose of tansy root. I even offered to gather some for her and tell your pa it was a tonic."

"She was scared of Pa," Rose said simply.

She went to stand close to the bed and look at Ma. It was as if she were seeing her for the first time. Ma's hawkish thin faces was relaxed and there seemed to be a tiny hint of a smile on it.

Rose looked at the lumpish stomach and wondered if the baby would have been a boy or a girl. Well, the baby was better off, too. It was better off to have gotten out of this world before it entered it. It was better off not to have Pa for a father.

Ellie and Buck did not make an appearance the evening of the wake. Probably because of the boys, Rose told herself. The boys needed their sleep but Ellie would surely come tomorrow.

She told Rebecca and Daniel of her visit to the Ansels, of how rude Buck had been and how awful Ellie had looked.

"Her eyes were all swollen and the little boys' faces were tear-stained.

"I'd like to give that big bully a taste of his own medicine," Daniel said.

"He's a killer," Rose cautioned. "Just stay away from him, Daniel. I begged Ellie not to marry him."

"I'm leaving soon," Daniel told his sisters now. "The only reason I stayed around was to help Ma. She's gone now and I'm getting out. Bree offered me ten dollars to sign a paper that he can have my share of the farm."

"He can have my share for free," Rebecca spoke up.

"Mine, too. He can have my share for free," Rose echoed.

"Well, I need the ten dollars to get away from here," Daniel said. "But I never want to see this old farm again."

"We all feel that way," Rose said. "All but Bree. It seems he feels he has to have the farm to somehow get even with Pa for all the beatings."

"Well, the old man has stropped me for the last time," Daniel said fervently.

"I hope so," Rose breathed. "I've suffered with you at every blow of that strop."

"Me, too," Rebecca said. "We love you so much, Daniel, and we'll miss you."

It rained the day of the funeral. It was a soft misty rain, the kind Rose remembered Sister Theresa having called "angel's tears."

The Dunn graveyard was at a far corner of the farm, on a desolate hillside that was apparently not suited for crops.

Their own ma had been buried there along with the four dead babies of their stepmother.

Daniel had often wanted to plant trees on that desolate strip of land, but Pa had forbidden him.

"It's all foolishness," he had declared angrily. "The dead don't know if they're layin' in shade or sun."

Rev. Timothy Falter spoke a few words at the grave side and the funeral was over.

Back at the farmhouse, a few of the neighbors

lingered to eat some of the food brought in for the wake. Others departed silently.

"What will happen now?" Rose asked Rebecca and Daniel that evening.

They looked at each other in silence.

Chapter 5

They did not have long to wait before they knew what was going to happen next.

Pa had gone off in the buckboard in the late afternoon. Rose was waiting to dish up supper on his return when she heard the buckboard and looked out the kitchen window to see Pa.

He had someone with him. A woman!

"Holy devil!" Bree snarled. "A woman! He wouldn't dare!"

"Our Pa would dare anything," Rebecca said matter-of-factly. "You know he brought Ma home shortly after our own mamma died."

He was helping the woman down from the seat of the buckboard.

"It's Mary Kahns," gasped Rose. "It can't be Mary Kahns."

They all knew Mary Kahns and knew of her reputation. She was a big woman with pendulous breasts, a horselike face, and bright red hair straggling down her back. She called herself a widow. She had a half-witted son about fifteen years old named Ira, and, together, they survived on a run-down farm. It was rumored she took on night visitors for added income.

The group in the kitchen watched their father and the woman walk toward the house. As they watched, a lad, as hefty as his mother, heaved himself from the back of the wagon and headed slowly toward the house.

In the kitchen, Pa announced simply, "Mrs. Kahns and Ira have come for supper."

Rebecca put two more plates on the table and Rose silently dished up the salt pork, potatoes, dandelion greens, and light bread.

The meal was eaten in silence broken only by grunts from Ira.

When they had finished eating, the two visitors, accompanied by Pa, left and the Dunns began to discuss the meaning of this strange unforeseen happening.

"That big lummox, Mary Kahns!" Bree snorted.

"You mean those two big lummoxes!" Daniel cried. "You don't suppose—"

Rose finished his unfinished sentence. "That Pa would bring her and that half-wit here?"

"I think Pa would do anything. I think if he could get her one hundred acres and have Ira as a free handyman and have the old woman for a bed partner he'd do it," Bree said shrewdly.

"Hush!" Rose said. "You shouldn't talk like that."

"Hell!" Bree rasped sharply. "We all know our Pa. We know that if he can get a woman like Mary Kahns, who is still pretty good-lookin', to bed with him he won't give a damn that Ma ain't cold in her grave yet."

"I don't care what he does; I'm getting out,"

Daniel said definitely.

"I'm goin' to stay right here and get what's mine. I want this farm and there ain't no red-headed whore like Mary Kahns goin' to get any part of it."

Rose sighed. She had no desire to live under the same roof with Mary Kahns and her slobbering son, Ira.

She and Rebecca would have to leave. Perhaps they could go away with Daniel.

Pa did not come home that night.

Rose lay in bed and thought of him and the buxom Mary Kahns locked in a sexual embrace and she shuddered at the thought.

She was heavy-hearted the next morning as she and Rebecca did their chores. She was worrying, too, about Ellie who had not come to Ma's funeral. But then, remembering Ellie's appearance, she could understand why she had not come. Poor Ellie!

As she and Rebecca gathered the eggs, they heard the sound of horses' hoofs. Someone was galloping at breakneck speed.

Rose's first thought was that something had happened to Ellie.

And then, rushing out of the barn, she saw a figure in white buckskin. The fringe on his suit danced and made him seem to be in perpetual motion.

It was George Newcomb. He grinned happily as he ran toward her.

Taking her in to his arms, he cried, "My

beautiful, beautiful Rose."

She clung to him. It was so good to see him again.

"You've come back," she said happily.

"Nothing could have kept me away from you, my darling. But you are upset about something. Tell me what it is," he urged.

"I expect Pa will be back at any moment, George."

"Good! I would like very much to meet the gentleman."

"Pa is no gentleman," Rose said matter-of-factly. "My sister, Ellie, married that no-good Buck Ansel and my ma died. Oh, George, so much has happened."

"Darling, if you don't want me to stay around now to meet your pa, can you slip out tonight and meet me? Then you can tell me what has happened," he suggested.

She told him of a place where they could meet. It was a clump of trees on the far hill; she had gone there since she was a child.

"Meet me this evening. Pa is courting and will no doubt be gone again tonight," she whispered.

"Courting!" the man echoed. "I thought you said your ma just died."

"Yes, that's right. Ma died and Pa brought a woman named Mary Kahns home for supper. He didn't come home last night. I guess he spent the night at her house. She's a tramp."

"Holy devil!" he exclaimed incredulously.

Rose was glancing nervously up the lane. It would never do for Pa to catch George here. He would be furious.

Seeing her nervousness and fear, he kissed her good-by.

Watching him gallop off up the lane, Rose breathed a sigh of relief.

Rebecca joined her now in the yard. "He's a fine figure of a man," she said admiringly.

"He's the handsomest man I've ever seen," Rose admitted.

"He loves you," Rebecca stated.

"I think I love him," Rose admitted, her cheeks flushing red as ripe fruit.

Pa came home presently. He said nothing to Rose or Rebecca. Bree and Daniel were in the fields working.

Rose carried their lunch to them and Bree asked if Pa had said anything about Mary Kahns.

"He didn't even say 'Good morning,' " Rose informed. "He didn't say a word."

"He didn't say nothin' to us either. I aim to ask him what he's goin' to do," Bree said belligerently.

"I wouldn't do that," Rose protested. "He might get awful mad."

"He's always mad anyway." Bree shrugged.

When the family gathered around the supper table that night, Rose hoped Bree had changed his mind about bringing up the subject of Mary Kahns.

But as Rose set out the food and the Dunns came silently to the table to eat, she saw the look of determination on Bree's sullen face and she knew he intended to ask Pa about Mary Kahns.

"Thought maybe you'd bring that woman and her crazy son to supper again," Bree drawled.

Pa glared at Bree.

"This is my house," Pa said after a deathly silence. "I can bring anyone I want to supper."

"She's a whore and I ain't got any hankerin' to eat supper with a whore," Bree growled.

Rose had never in her wildest dreams thought Bree or anyone else for that matter, would speak to Pa in this fashion.

Pa seemed frozen with anger. Then he pushed his plate back. His face was black with rage as he started for the strop hanging by the door.

"You're goin' to get the beatin' of your life," Pa growled.

Rose and Rebecca were trembling.

Bree stood up. "You'll not touch me, old man. You've beaten me for the last time. I'll kill you if you ever try to strop me again."

Pa looked Bree up and down and evidently, for the first time, realized that Bree was now a full-grown man. He cussed and stormed out of the kitchen and presently the four Dunns heard the buckboard going up the lane.

"You stood up to him," Daniel cried in admiration.

"You can stand up to him, too, when you get as big as me. He's just a big bully. I get raving mad when I think how many times he's clobbered me through the years. I've gone to bed many a time all bloody from him beatin' me," Bree noted and his voice was rough with hatred.

"What will happen now?" Rose asked.

"I guess he's gone off to Mary Kahns," Rebecca said.

"Wish he'd stay there," Daniel cried. "We can sure do without him here."

"He'll spend the night in Mary's bed," Bree jeered. "What a pair they make!"

Chapter 6

The night was moon-washed with silver as Rose hurried down the lane and cut across the field to her secret woodland room.

She turned back once to look at the old farmhouse. Old and weather-beaten, it looked mystically beautiful in the silver glow; even the towering trees, the bushes, and the daisies were silver-tipped and shining.

Would Pa return on the morrow? She wondered as she hurried to meet George, and would he still be angry because Bree had called Mary Kahns a whore?

Well, she was a whore, Rose reasoned to herself. At least, local gossip said she was a whore. But she had to admit to herself that Mary with her lush figure would appeal to a man. Especially a man like Pa!

George was waiting and swept her into his arms.

"My beautiful Rose," he cried. "I could hardly wait until you got here. I was afraid your pa had kept you from coming."

She told him then of Bree's encounter with Pa at the supper table.

George whooped with laughter. "You mean

that big brother of yours actually called her a whore?"

"Yes, but I don't think it's so funny." she said slightly miffed.

"It is funny, my sweetheart. Here your pa brings home his lady love and your brother has the guts to call her a whore!" And he went off again into peals of laughter.

"She's got a half-witted son, too, and he's got a mean look in his eye," Rose went on.

"You don't suppose your pa will bring this woman and her son to your house to live?"

"I don't know," Rose answered. "I hope not. She's a great big woman with red hair."

"And your pa stays all night at her house?" George questioned.

"He stayed last night and I'm sure he'll stay there tonight. He went off very angry after Bree called her a whore," she went on. "Pa was going to strop Bree, but Bree stood up to him. Pa has stropped Bree and Daniel since they were little boys, but this time Bree stood up to him."

"Did he ever strop you girls?" he asked curiously.

"No, he never stropped us. But he has always handy about whipping us with a big stick he kept close by. Sometimes I thought he wanted to kill us," she said.

"My poor Rose," he whispered cradling her in his arms.

Presently he spoke again. "And you said your ma died and Ellie got married to the man that bid fifty cents on her box at the box social?"

"Yes, poor Ma died. She was just worn out and she just gave up. At least she's at rest now."

"And Ellie?"

"I tried and tried to get Ellie to give up the idea of marrying up with that no-good Buck Ansel. But she was determined. I think she felt awful sorry for his two boys, Link and Hank," she explained.

"But that's no reason to marry a brute like him," George exclaimed. "If he's cruel to those boys he's going to be cruel to her."

"I tried to tell her that, but it was no use. She just wouldn't listen. He didn't want to have a marriage party either, but I said she was Ellie Dunn and she would have a marriage party. He couldn't tell her what to do until she was his wife."

"He didn't like that, I guess."

"He was mad about it, but Rebecca and I had Rev. Timothy Falter come. Daniel gathered roses for the bride's bouquet and hair and big pink mallows for the tables for the spread afterward."

"Sounds like you had a real party."

"Yes, but, George, Buck dragged Ellie off as soon as the ceremony was over. I offered to keep the boys so Buck and Ellie could have a honeymoon," she related.

"And what did old Buck say to that?"

"He yelled, 'Honeymoon! Hell! Who needs a honeymoon? There's work to be done.' "

"What a fool he is!" George exclaimed. "What a dumb blind fool!"

"And George, when I rode over to their house to tell them of Ma's death, Ellie came to the door and she was all beat up. I told you about that, didn't I?"

"Not in detail, my sweet. You've had a terrible time," he said sympathetically.

"Ellie didn't come to Ma's funeral. She loved Ma and I know she would have come if Buck would have let her. Of course, she looked awful, all bruised up. Maybe she didn't want folks to see her looking like that."

He held her close now and his lips went to hers, tenderly.

"My poor, brave sweetheart," he whispered as he kissed her again and again.

She relaxed in his arms.

Presently he put a hand to her breast.

She jerked away trembling.

"What is it, Rose?" he questioned. "I want only to feel your loveliness."

"I . . . I can't let you touch me," she faltered.

"Rose, you evidently have the wrong idea about love," he said gently. "You've gotten the wrong idea from hearing your pa. Is that right?"

"Yes, oh yes," she whispered. "George all my life I've had to listen to Pa rooting around like a pig at night and to Ma submitting."

"That isn't real love, my sweetheart. I will teach you about real love," he asserted.

She relaxed again in his arms.

"We will take it one step at a time and I will be gentle with you, Here, let me touch one of your sweet breasts. I touch it with love, my dearest," he said, tenderly stroking her breasts, one at a time.

After a while she said she must go, and he reluctantly stopped his soft stroking.

"Tomorrow night, we will take another step,"

he promised kissing her good night.

Pa swaggered into the farmhouse in the morning. He ate a hearty breakfast and said nary a word to anyone.

That evening after supper he left again and all the Dunns breathed easier. It was good to have him away.

Rose again went to their meeting place to see George.

Again, he stroked her breasts until finally she whispered, "That makes me feel strange."

"That strange feeling is the beginning of desire," he explained.

"Desire?" she questioned.

"Sweetheart, to feel desire is a wonderful feeling," he instructed. "Your natural feelings have been buried under disgust and fear. I intend to melt that ice that has covered your heart."

"I love you, George," she whispered.

"And I love you," he answered fervently. He began to unbutton her dress, then pushed back the heavy homemade straps of her petticoats until her breasts were exposed.

"I shouldn't let you do this," she murmured.

"But you want me to," he prompted.

"Yes, oh, yes," she cried. "Don't stop now."

"I shan't stop, my beautiful Rose. I'm going to make you squirm with desire."

He fondled an amber-tipped breast and then bent down to kiss it, first one and then the other.

"Oh, George," she murmured and began to cry. Her hands came up and touched his face, then she put her arms around his neck and clung to him.

He pushed her away for a moment and looked at the beauty of her breasts rising like plump ripe pears.

"My darling," he murmured and put his lips again to her breasts, playing and nuzzling and nibbling while she moaned and whimpered.

Her knees sagged and he drew her gently down to the moss-covered earth.

"I can't stand it," she whispered.

"Darling, I told you we would take one step at a time."

"I . . . I hurt down below," she faltered. "I feel strange down below."

"That is because you want me in you," he whispered.

"Oh, George," she murmured weakly. "That would be wrong."

"It is not wrong when two people love each other," he said definitely.

"I'm a virgin," she said proudly.

"I know, my sweetheart, I know. That is why we are taking it one step at a time. Tomorrow evening we will take another step."

She could hardly wait for Pa to leave the farmhouse after supper. George was waiting and was going to take her one step further toward ecstasy.

It was hard to understand how George's kisses could be so wonderful, could make her swim in a sort of radiance. It was heavenly, too, when he felt her breasts and kissed and fondled them, but the memory of Pa's touching her breasts still filled her with revulsion.

When she reached their secret place, George was already there. He took her in his arms. She told him then of how Pa had grabbed her in the barn and how even the very thought yet sickened her.

"That is all in the past," he comforted. "Your idea of love is all made new in our love. Come, tonight we will take the next step."

Again he fondled her breasts, nibbling and kissing each one.

"Harder," she begged. "Suck me harder."

"I do not want to hurt you," he murmured.

"Make me feel that I'm alive," she cried passionately. "Hurt me. Suck hard."

"Yes, my darling."

He opened his shirt to his navel and she kissed his neck and his chest. Then he gently pulled her to the earth as on the previous evening.

But this time, he began to undress her, and when she lay naked in his arms with the moonlight streaming through the trees and making a lacy pattern on her alabaster skin, he caressed the insides of her thighs.

Ecstasy surged through her and she trembled with passion.

"Take me," she begged.

He forced her beneath him and he sought to enter her.

She groaned and caught her breath sharply.

"I will be gentle, my darling," he whispered. "Just let go and think of our love."

She relaxed and he forced himself into her.

She stiffened for a moment—the pain was in-

47

tense—and then she began to move with him in a slow rocking, rising, and falling motion.

Tears hung in the corners of her green eyes, but her beautiful face glowed with passion and love for him.

They reached the heights of ecstasy together and when it was over and he had rolled off her, they looked at each other in the moonlight.

"Now you belong to me," he said firmly. "I have taken your maidenhead and you are mine."

"I am glad I belong to you, George," she whispered happily. "Oh, I'm so glad I belong to you."

Chapter 7

Every evening, she experienced ecstasy. She could endure the boredom of the long summer days only because she knew that George was waiting for her in their secret woodland room.

Pa continued to visit Mary Kahns every night. He was sullen and glowered at Bree, but said nothing to him. Bree, in turn, frowned and grumbled.

Daniel was impatient for Bree to give him the promised ten dollars so he could be off. And Rebecca worried constantly about the possibility of Pa bringing Mary Kahns and Ira to live with them.

As for Rose, she lived in a world of daydreams and happiness. She thought of George constantly. She did not dream too much of the future; she was content with the present.

But one evening when they had scaled the heights to intense rapture, she asked, "What if I should get in the family way, George?"

He answered promptly, "Then we will get married."

She shuddered at the word, *marriage*.

"But darling, all marriages aren't like your pa's,

or like Ellie's" he protested.

"I know, but when I think of marriage I think of them. It's horrible."

"You know how sweet love can be," he explained gently. "Of course, there's always tansy."

"I used to wonder why Ma didn't take tansy," Rose said now as she lay cuddled in George's arms.

"Probably scared of your Pa," George answered simply. "Fear is a terrible thing, Rose."

"Have you ever been afraid?" she asked.

"Many times. I've had some rough times."

"Tell me what you do, George. You've never said."

"I'll tell you all about it one of these days soon," he promised.

"I love you so much, George," she breathed.

"You are ready again?" he asked, teasingly.

"I'm always ready."

"You amaze me, my darling. Especially so, since you were a virgin when I first entered you."

"You didn't mind the blood?" she queried.

"Sweetheart, I knew you were a virgin from your actions, but the blood really told me so," he observed.

"It hurt badly."

"But it was a sweet kind of hurt, wasn't it?"

"Oh, yes, George, yes. And now I can't get enough of our being together like this. I dream of our joy in each other every moment that we are separated."

"My dearest," he whispered and took her again.

When their rapture had subsided and they lay cradled in each other's arms, he said, "Dearest, I have to go away for a little while."

"No," she cried. "I can't do without you. Don't go away."

"It will only be for a week or so. Doolin has it all planned and I have to go."

"Who is Doolin?" she asked.

"He's my boss," George answered.

"What kind of a boss?"

He kissed her hard. "Don't ask too many questions."

"But I want to know," she said firmly. "I want to know everything about you."

"And you shall know everything soon," he promised. "When I return I'll answer any questions you might ask."

This pleased her and she ran her fingers lovingly over his navel.

"More?" he asked.

"More and more and more," she answered jutting up a young firm breast for him to kiss.

It started to rain that night. The heavy drops beat hard against the windows. Lightning flashed and thunder roared.

"I'm afraid, Rose," Rebecca whispered.

They were in bed. Rose patted her sister, trying to comfort her.

"You were never afraid of storms before," she pointed out. "This storm is no different from thousands of other storms."

"I don't know why, Rose, but I feel that something awful is going to happen." Rebecca groaned. "Do you suppose Pa is going to bring that awful woman home with him?"

"Honey, you worry about that all the time. If he was going to bring her home, I think he would have brought her home by now."

"Wouldn't that be awful? Wouldn't that be perfectly awful if he brought that red-haired woman here. I'm afraid of that crazy Ira."

"Don't worry about it," Rose comforted. "Pa wouldn't be that foolish.

But Rose was wrong!

The next morning Pa came into the yard with Mary Kahns and Ira on the seat beside him, the wagon was piled high with furniture and bedding.

Bree and Daniel were already in the fields, but Rose and Rebecca remained glued by astonishment, at the door.

"Help with the unloadin'," Pa growled.

The girls went forward woodenly.

Ira stood watching, slobbering as he grinned, and making no effort to help.

Mary went into the house.

Rose, struggling with a large rocker, asked, "Where shall I put this rocker, Pa?"

"Mary will tell you where," he said brusquely.

When Rose pulled the rocker into the house, she saw the woman going from room to room as if surveying her castle.

Rebecca, in the process of pulling a small table off the buckboard, asked Pa, "Is that woman really going to move in with us?"

"She's goin' to be my housekeeper," the man snarled. "Now get a move on. It's startin' to rain again."

"Why doesn't that crazy Ira help? He's strong and—"

Rebecca's question was never finished. Pa came forward quickly and hit her with all his strength across her mouth.

Blood spurted as she flew through the air.

"Ha, ha," laughed Ira dancing around in glee.

Hearing the commotion, Rose and Mary came out of the house. Rose hurried to pick Rebecca up.

"Shut up that cryin'," Pa boomed at Rebecca, "or I'll give you somethin' to cry about."

"What did she do?" Mary giggled. "What did she do? Did she sass you?"

Pa ignored her questions, but advanced menacingly toward Rebecca. Rose stepped in front of her sister and faced Pa.

"Don't you hit her again," she cried.

"Ain't never stropped you, but I can do it," Pa growled.

"You wouldn't dare," Rose cried angrily.

The man grabbed Rose by the arm, and pulling her after him, went into the kitchen where he got the strop off the wall.

Rebecca followed, crying and moaning.

"Whop her good," Mary squealed in delight. "Make her strip down and give it to her good."

"I do my stropping in the woodshed," Pa exclaimed.

Rose jerked back, but Pa pulled her roughly toward the shed.

"Wanna watch," Ira jabbered.

"Go and watch," the mother put in. "I want to watch too. I like to see someone get a real whipping. Strop her hard, James. I'm goin' to like this."

In the woodshed, long ago Pa had hammered a stick of wood like a handlebar to the wall.

"Grab it girl," Pa commanded belligerently.

Ira was dancing around in glee.

This can't be happening to me, Rose thought. This must be a nightmare: Pa telling her to hang onto the whipping handle, this strange, fat red-haired woman ogling her, and Ira with his slobbering mouth open in delight!

If only George would come! George would take her away.

Pa reared back his arm and brought the strop down across her back.

The pain seared her like a hot iron.

"Harder," shrieked Mary.

"Stop it, stop it," Rebecca cried flinging herself between the strop and Rose.

Then there was the quick shuffle of footsteps at the door of the woodshed and Bree and Daniel came in.

"What's goin' on here?" Bree demanded.

"What the hell do you think is goin' on?" Pa yelled angrily. "Rose is getting a whippin'."

Daniel had jumped to Rose's side and was drawing her away from the projected whipping stick.

Rose saw that he was angrier than she had ever seen before in his life.

Bree was staring at the woman and her son and now demanded, "What the hell are they doing here?"

"They've come here to live," Pa said roughly.

"Did you marry up with her?" Bree asked.

"She's goin' to be my housekeeper." Pa smirked brazenly.

"Housekeeper!" Bree echoed. "You mean she's goin' to be your damned whore."

Pa reared back his arm; his hand still held the strop.

Bree jumped aside.

"That no-good wench ain't goin' to live under the same roof as us Dunns."

"This here's my house, and what I say goes," Pa asserted.

"That hag will wish she'd never set foot in this farmhouse," Bree said darkly as the group started to the house.

"Thought I was goin' to see a real beatin'," Ira mourned.

Daniel was instructed by Pa to unload the rest of the furniture, and Bree stared at Mary and Ira with hate.

There was one large welt across Rose's back which Rebecca treated with grease, rubbing gently.

"We can't stay here," Rebecca whispered. "Maybe we can leave with Daniel."

"Yes, we'll have to leave. Did you hear that horrible woman actually goading Pa on? And that slobbering half-wit laughing with joy because I was being whipped?"

"Yes, yes, I heard."

When it was finally time to go to bed, the woman went boldly into Pa's room.

Rose and Rebecca strained to hear. They heard

loud laughter and wrestling around.

Then finally, Pa was rooting and groaning and moaning and the woman's high tinkling laugh rang out.

After a while they heard her yell, "Leave me alone. Enough is enough."

She sounded mean.

"She's tough," Rebecca whispered. "She's not like poor Ma."

"Good," Rose whispered. "They're two of a kind. They deserve each other."

"I'm afraid of that Ira. He's sleeping on a cot in front of the fireplace. And he's up to no good."

"Let's talk to Daniel tomorrow. Maybe he'll take us with him. You did think maybe he would take us with him. Regardless, we've got to get out of here; but first, I have to see George."

"When will he be back?"

"In a week or two."

"That's an awfully long time to stay here with those two monsters," Rebecca mourned.

Chapter 8

In the old farmhouse, there was an intense feeling of hatred. Mary Kahns, in her role of housekeeper, barked orders at Rose and Rebecca, while Ira lounged around, slobbering and spying on the girls.

The days dragged by. Rose was on fire from wanting George's touch on her body. She ached for him.

Daniel was anxious to be off, but Bree could not produce the promised ten dollars and Daniel could not leave without the money.

Rose and Rebecca had approached Daniel about their desire to leave with him, he had reluctantly agreed to their plan.

Bree was badgering Pa for the money he owed him but Pa was in a meaner mood than usual. Apparently Mary Kahns lush body did not hold the enticements he had anticipated, and she was not as docile a partner as Ma had been. Then, one evening after the evening meal, Pa, with much ceremony, paid Bree his pittance.

Daniel's eyes sparkled. He would leave in the morning.

Rose and Rebecca looked at each other. Rose

knew she could not leave without telling George — and George had not returned!

Ira followed Bree and Daniel outside and watched as Bree gave his brother the money; then he immediately dashed inside whimpering. "Big boy give other boy money."

Rose's first thought was that they had underestimated Ira's intelligence. He wasn't as dumb as he appeared and acted.

"Big boy give other boy money," Ira was shrieking now, knowing that he had everyone's attention.

Pa had risen from his place by the front window and, his face black with wrath, he rushed outside.

Daniel had the money in his pocket, but was busily signing a piece of paper proffered by Bree. Pa jerked the paper away and demanded the money.

"It's my money," Bree asserted stubbornly. "It's my money and I gave it to Daniel."

"Give it to me, boy," Pa commanded.

"I won't," Daniel said boldly, firmly.

"I'll skin you alive," the man shouted and jerked Daniel toward the woodshed.

"He'll kill him, Rebecca," Rose moaned. "We've got to do something."

And then a voice, blessedly familiar to Rose, cracked across the group.

"What the hell," it blazed, "is going on here?"

It was George! Rose raced to his side.

"Oh, George, George. You've come back."

"And just in time, it seems."

"Pa is going to beat Daniel because Daniel won't

give him the money Bree gave him," she explained breathlessly.

Pa faced the stranger angrily. "Who the blazes are you? And what business is it of yours? This is my place and you'd better damned well get off of it."

"Let me introduce myself, sir," George said calmly. "I am your daughter Rose's friend."

"Get the hell out of here. Rose has no friends unless I say so," Pa boomed.

"Quit your bellering," George demanded.

Pa apparently decided to ignore him and began to drag Daniel away.

"Don't let him strop Daniel," Rose cried, clutching George. "He almost kills him when he beats him."

"He won't beat him, dear," George spoke tenderly. "I'll take care of this."

He said nothing more as he took Rose's hand in his and followed Pa and Daniel.

Everyone trailed behind. Mary Kahns and Ira were livid with excitement.

"Now tell me what happened?" George instructed Rose as they walked.

Rose told him of how Pa had stropped her and how Pa had brought Mary Kahns and her half-witted son home to live and the misery that had brought.

She told how Bree had given Daniel ten dollars to go away from the farm and how Daniel had signed a paper that gave Bree his share of the farm.

George listened intently as he and Rose trailed

into the woodshed. Pa had stepped into the kitchen for the strop and he came out now swinging it back and forth.

But George spoke. "Daniel, I understand that you would like to leave this farm."

"Yes," Daniel said.

"Then you shall," George said as he drew his Colt from his holster. "Is there anything you would like to do before you leave?"

Daniel looked at Pa with hate bright in his eyes.

"Yes, I would like to strop Pa as he has stropped me through all these years."

"Then you shall, Daniel," George said definitely. "Take the strop and you, old man, grab that stick there. I suppose that is what you made your victims hang on to."

Pa began to scream oaths at George, but George, with the Colt focused on Pa, calmly took the strop and handed it to Daniel.

"He's all yours," he said generously. "Beat him as hard and as long as you like."

Daniel grinned. "I've wanted to do this ever since I was knee-high."

He reared back his arm and brought it down hard on Pa's back—again and again and again.

The man screamed. He groaned. He moaned and cussed. But Daniel persisted.

Then he stopped a moment to ask, "How does it feel, Pa? How does it feel to have your back on fire with pain? Sometimes you would beat me night after night and I would want to die. Now you'll get a taste of what it's like."

Finally George called a halt.

"You have your money, Daniel?" George asked.

Daniel nodded as he watched Pa writhe with pain.

"Here is more money," George said, taking some from his pocket. "You have a horse?"

"Yes. I have Nellie."

"Then go and may good luck go with you."

Daniel looked at Rose and Rebecca.

"Don't worry about your sisters. I will take care of them," George promised.

Daniel hurriedly kissed Rose and Rebecca, and cast a parting glance at Pa who was moaning and groaning on the dirt floor of the woodshed.

With a quick good-by to Bree and George, he was gone and presently, they heard the horses' hoofs clattering away.

"Gather your things together," George instructed Rose and Rebecca, "and let's be off."

"You can't go," Mary screamed at the girls. "Who will do the work?"

"You can do your own work from now on," George hissed.

Rose and Rebecca soon joined George. Each had a tiny bundle, for their possessions were few.

"Luckily I brought an extra horse," George said. "I came intending to talk to your pa tonight. It was lucky I came at the right moment."

"Oh, George," Rose whispered, "I love you."

Chapter 9

A whole new world and life awaited Rose in Ingalls. George took her and Rebecca to the hotel in the town and introduced them to its owner, Kate Meadows.

Immediately, Kate enthusiastically hugged the two girls.

Rose had an impression of uncorseted softness, violet water, blondish-gray hair curling above a soft powdered face, and magnificent eyes filled with affection and amusement.

"You beauties!" she cried "George, you must have found the two prettiest girls in Oklahoma."

"They need a place to stay, Kate," he explained.

"Got two real nice rooms just waiting for them." The woman beamed.

"Could you use some help around the hotel for a while?" he asked.

"Sure could. There's plenty of work around here and I'd like to have some help. How about some grub right now?"

George led the way to an adjoining room where there were many tables covered with red-checkered cloths.

As they ate, George and Kate kept up a constant

banter. It was plain that they enjoyed each other's company.

"Kate was once known as the Toast of the West Coast," George related.

"And I was once Queen of the Barbary Coast," the woman said proudly.

"And a beauty," the man teased. "But then, you'll always be a beauty."

The woman beamed, pleased."

The room, which Kate presently showed her, was small but neat. Rebecca's room was across the hall and the two girls could only express amazement and delight.

Asleep in her bed that night, Rose awakened to marvel at the sudden change in her life. She was actually asleep in a bed alone. She stretched luxuriously. And best of all, she was free of Pa and that strop hanging by the door. Free, too, of fat Mary Kahns and slobbering Ira. And Daniel was free, and on his way to adventure.

The next day, Kate took Rose and Rebecca to Marsh's General Store and bought each of them several dresses.

"But we don't have any money," Rose objected. "You should wait until we earn some working for you."

"Nonsense." The woman laughed. "I'll take it out of your wages. Tell you a secret, though. George wanted to give me some money for you two. But it ain't proper for young ladies to be takin' money from a gentleman."

The work on the farm had been hard. There had been endless chores to be done. They had worked from dawn until dark. But here at the hotel, Rose thought everything was fun. She and Rebecca took turns registering guests; they made beds; they swept and sometimes they scrubbed.

George had left on one of his mysterious trips and Rose was anxious for him to return so she could show off her new dresses. She thought of the loose-fitting dresses, made of flour sacks, that she had worn on the farm. She had never in all her life had more than one good Sunday-go-to-meeting dress.

She asked Kate where George went when he went off like this.

Kate looked at her in surprise.

"You honestly don't know?" she queried in amazement.

"No."

"Have you ever heard of Doolin?"

"George mentioned him one time and said he was his boss."

Kate laughed merrily. "That he is," she said.

"George promised to tell me more, but he never got around to it," Rose explained. "So much happened so quickly."

"Well, when Doolin's boys get to town next week we're going to have a real party. You've seen the big room at the back of the hotel where town meetings are held? Well, that's where we're going to have the party."

"What kind of a party?"

"You ain't never seen a party like this. We have 'em every time the gang comes in after a big job. A real shindig!"

"I can hardly wait."

"Then you ain't met Bill Doolin?" Kate asked.

"No."

"Then you've got a real treat in store for you," Kate promised. "Next to your man, George, there ain't no one like that Bill Doolin. He can charm a rattlesnake if he wants. He's not as good-lookin' as George, but he's mighty pleasin' to see."

"Are Bill Doolin and George good friends?" Rose asked.

"Honey, they would lay down their lives for each other," Kate said solemnly.

Rose felt a quick twinge of jealousy.

"Bill Doolin came up the hard way," Kate said admiringly. "His pa was an Arkansas cotton farmer and Bill left home when he was about fifteen to wander about the West, working as a ranch hand. George met Bill at Oscar Halsell's H X Bar Ranch on the Cimarron River."

"And they've been friends for a long time?" Rose asked.

"Yes, and I've jabbered enough. Let's straighten up that back room. Those boys might ride in any time."

Chapter 10

When Kate Meadows had said the party for the returning Doolin Gang would be a shindig, that's what she'd meant!

The men swarmed down upon the hotel one evening whooping and yelling.

Rose was waiting for George and he took her instantly in his arms and held her close.

"My beautiful Rose," he whispered. "I could hardly wait to come back to you."

"Are all these men part of Doolin's gang?" she asked.

"Rose, you are absolutely beautiful in that pink-checked dress," he said, abruptly changing the subject.

"You don't want to talk about Doolin's gang now, is that it?" she asked, piqued.

"When we have time I will tell you everything you need to know," he promised. "Come, I want you to meet Bill Doolin."

Rose was never to forget her first meeting with the leader of the gang.

He had dark curly hair, hazel eyes, and a handlebar mustache.

He was smiling at her. "Ah," he breathed softly,

"I heard how very beautiful you are and the compliment has not been exaggerated. Bitter Creek, you are a lucky man."

When Bill Doolin eventually drifted away, Rose asked, "What did he call you?"

"Bitter Creek. That's what the gang calls me," he explained.

And now the gang came to be introduced. There were so many men and their names were so confusing that Rose wondered if she would ever remember any of them.

Afterward, she remembered Red Buck, Little Dick, Tulsa Jack, Dynamite Dick, and Charley Pierce—obviously an Indian—Arkansas Tom and Little Bill.

They seemed to be cut from the same mold. They all moved quickly, their eyes were sharp, and their skin was burned brown by the sun.

There must have been between forty and fifty men in all, and when Bill Doolin began to play his fiddle, Rose thought for a moment that all of the men rushed toward her demanding the first dance.

She made the excuse that she did not know how to dance. But they laughed that excuse aside and she found herself being passed from one set of very masculine arms to another.

It was all fun and terribly exciting. Rose looked for Rebecca in the crowd, but could not find her.

She saw Kate Meadows dancing with one of the gang. She was evidently having a great time. Her huge uncorseted figure was bobbing up and down in time to the music and her eyes were sparkling.

Rose finally found herself in George's arms.

"I'll be with you tonight," he whispered.

"But how can you?" she whispered back.

"This party will go on and on and most of the men will be pretty well liquored up by the time its over. They'll be wandering up and down the halls and having a hell of a time."

She was jerked from George's arms by Little Dick.

"Where did that lucky Bitter Creek find a beauty like you?" he asked.

"I lived on a farm," she explained. "He came to a—"

The sentence was never finished because she was snatched away by Red Buck who was slightly unsteady on his feet.

The party went on and on. Presently Red Buck, really drunk by now, tried to shoot out the lamps, but Tulsa Jack stopped his pastime and persuaded him to dance with the widow, Mae Ames, who helped out in the hotel dining room and was anxiously trying to acquire a new husband. Red Buck hobbled around, staggering to and fro, while the Widow Mae tried valiantly to hold him up.

Presently Rose was in George's arms again and he was guiding her out the door. They hurried up the stairs to her room.

Once there, he held her close. "At last," he breathed. "At last we are together again. Tonight you will be mine again."

"I missed you, too," she whispered. "I missed you terribly."

"From now on, I want you to call me Bitter Creek," he told her as he started to undress.

"It will be hard for me to get used to calling you Bitter Creek."

He laughed.

"You'll get used to it," he assured her.

"I want to see if Rebecca is in her room," she said suddenly. "I'll be back in a moment."

She slipped across the hall and opened the door to Rebecca's room.

From the light of the moon trickling into the room, Rose could see her sister, sound asleep.

She went back to her room slightly puzzled.

"George, I mean Bitter Creek, I didn't see Rebecca dancing," she said slowly. "I wonder if she didn't stay at the party."

"Maybe she doesn't like parties."

In bed, she gave herself completely to Bitter Creek.

They loved with wild abandon.

He sucked and fondled her breasts until she squirmed with mad desire.

And when he entered her, she was dazzled with desire for him.

Afterward, she asked simply, "Have you had many women, Bitter Creek?"

For a moment, he did not answer. When he spoke it was to ask, "Do you want the truth?"

"I want us never to lie to each other," she said.

"Yes, I have had many women." He spoke sincerely. "You see, dearest, an outlaw lives for the moment. We are the quick and the dead and we know it."

"Oh, Bitter Creek," she moaned.

"Dance-hall girls are a dime a dozen," he went on. "But Rose, I swear to you that from this moment on I will be true to you."

They loved again and this time when she gave her body to him she felt a difference. She felt that now he truly belonged to her.

The gang remained for several weeks in Ingalls. During this time, Bill Doolin planned their next robbery, and Bitter Creek told Rose much about the Doolin gang.

"When the territory was opened and the H X Bar was abandoned, Bill Doolin and I split up. He drifted south to join Bob Dalton, whom he had met up with somewhere along the way."

"I've heard about the Daltons," Rose murmured.

"Who hasn't?" Bitter Creek asked. "Bill rode with the Daltons in a daring holdup of a train at Red Rock, a station on the Santa Fe, a few miles north of Perry, Oklahoma."

"I remember Bree saying something about the Dalton gang having a reign of terror," Rose put in.

"That's right, darling. You know Bob Dalton was once a Deputy United States Marshal and also police chief of the Osage Nation. Well, the gang rode from one end of the southwest to the other—robbing trains, and banks, and stealing large numbers of horses. They were smart. They would use relays of horses to escape into 'The Nations,' where the law of the white man could not reach."

"I'm glad you didn't go with Bill when you left the H X Bar."

"That was right smart of me," he agreed.

"Bob Dalton had planned to rob the two banks at Coffeyville, Kansas. But the people of Dalton fooled them and the plan ended in disaster. Bill's horse went lame a short distance from Coffeyville and he was saved because of that. Lucky Bill Doolin!"

"And lucky Bitter Creek Newcomb!" Rose cried thankfully.

"We've got a good gang," he went on presently. "They come from all parts of the West. They know Hell's Fringe—the Oklahoma badlands—as well as they know the backs of their own hands."

"Is Ingalls your headquarters?" she asked.

"Yes, and we've got two hideouts: the famous Creek Nation Cave—a few miles west—and Old Rock Fort Ranch."

"I'll worry about you, Bitter Creek, now that I know you are part of the Doolin gang."

"Not part of it, dearest. I'm the first lieutenant," he boasted.

"You see, Doolin heard of the massacre at Coffeyville and with a price of five thousand dollars on his head, he rode day and night until he reached Old Rock Fort. There he got a gang together and that's when I joined."

Rose kissed him. "I love you," she whispered.

"Our first robbery was successful. The vault of the First National Bank at Spearville in Ford County, Kansas, was cleaned of every dollar. We were always lucky."

Chapter 11

Every night there was a party in the big room at the back of the hotel, but Rebecca refused to attend.

"I don't like that wild kind of dancing," she said.

"It's fun," Rose said.

"You won't be angry, Rose, if I tell you I wrote Bill Eckridge?"

Rose was shocked. "Don't you like it here?" she cried.

"Yes."

"You don't want to go back to the farm again, do you? You don't want to see Pa and Mary and Ira?" she demanded.

"No, not them; but I miss Bill. I just thought he might come here and see me."

Rose sighed. "I know you always liked Bill. I think that would be fine if he would come here and see you. You could have a nice visit," she said.

"I wonder how things are at home, Rose," Rebecca said slowly. "I wonder how Bree is getting along. Maybe Bill can tell us."

"I'm curious, too," Rose acknowledged. "But, honey, I would really miss you if you went away."

"I'm not going anywhere. Bill would never ask me to go away with him," she said sadly.

When Bill came, he seemed young and awkward compared to the gang, who had departed on a robbery planned by their leader, Bill Doolin.

Rose and Rebecca plied him with questions.

He had seen Bree at the mill. Bree had been sullen and uncommunicative, as usual.

He had remarked that Mary Kahns was a whore and he hated her and her half-witted son, Ira.

"And Pa?" Rose questioned. "Did he mention Pa?"

"Said the old devil was as mean as ever," Bill said, flushing.

Rose laughed.

Rebecca was beside herself with joy at seeing Bill again. Her face glowed with happiness.

When he left, he asked if he might come again.

"Of course," Rose replied. "Come anytime you can."

"Do you think he'll come back again?" Rebecca questioned later.

"Wild horses couldn't keep him away," Rose assured her.

After that, Bill Eckridge came about every other week.

When the gang returned, successful as usual, Rose was so engrossed with pleasing Bitter Creek and enjoying the nightly dances, that it was almost a shock when Rebecca, her face the color of roses, came to announce that Bill Eckridge had asked her to marry him.

"Where will you live?" she asked.

"Bill's folks will let us live in their soddy," Rebecca said happily.

"But will you be happy in a soddy after living like this?" Rose asked, gesturing to their surroundings now.

"I would be happy living with Bill in a cave," Rebecca asserted. "Oh, Rose, be happy for me."

"I *am* happy for you," Rose said. "I just never thought about you getting married so quickly."

Rebecca laughed. "I can hardly wait to be married to Bill. I love him so much."

"You can be married here in Ingalls and we can have a big party here afterward," Rose planned.

"Oh, no, Rose. Bill wants to be married in the church at home by Rev. Falter."

"That's fine," Rose said. "We'll all come. The whole gang will come."

"No, just you and Bitter Creek and Kate come," Rebecca said quickly. "I'm afraid Ma and Pa Eckridge wouldn't take kindly to Tulsa Jack or Red Buck or some of the others."

Rose laughed. "I guess you're right," she agreed. "And probably the reverend wouldn't appreciate forty whooping and howling men."

Kate generously insisted on buying Rebecca's wedding dress and also the dress to be worn by Rose who would serve as bridesmaid.

"Are you going to invite Pa and Bree?" Rose asked. "Oh, and we have to get word to Ellie. She must come."

"Bill is going by Pa's place to invite him and

Bree, and he'll also go by Ellie's," Rebecca answered happily.

"Wouldn't it be awful if Mary Kahns and Ira decide to come?" Rose asked.

"Well, anyone can come to the church, Rose, but Mary and Ira aren't invited to the wedding party at the Eckridges'."

"I'm so anxious to see Ellie again," Rose cried. "It will be so nice for the three Dunn sisters to be together. I wish Daniel were here. Remember how he gathered roses for Ellie's bouquet?"

"And pink mallows for the tables?"

Chapter 12

It was a perfect day for a wedding—bright and sunshiny and full of the scent of flowers wafted by soft breezes.

The church was filled to overflowing. Everyone had loved Rebecca and the Eckridges' were well liked by their neighbors.

Rebecca and Rose looked so beautiful in their new gowns that Bitter Creek and Kate were lavish in their praise.

The Rev. Timothy Falter was in his usual good form, and as the music drifted from the old pump organ, Rose whispered to the radiant Rebecca, "May you always be as happy as you are now."

As Rebecca, Bill, Rose, and Bill's brother, Henry, turned to wend their way up the aisle after the ceremony, Rose looked for Ellie. She saw Pa and Bree and she smiled at them. Then she saw Mary Kahns and Ira sitting close to Pa—but not Ellie.

It was a happy gathering at the Eckridges'. The tables were loaded with food and Grandpa Ezra Riggs had brought his fiddle. The afternoon was a joyous time and Rose enjoyed seeing old friends and neighbors, although neither Pa nor Bree came to the wedding party.

"I'm worried about Ellie not coming to Rebecca's wedding," Rose told Bitter Creek. "Sweetheart, would you take me by her place on our way back to Ingalls?"

"Of course," he agreed. "I'm curious, too, as to why she wouldn't come to her own sister's wedding."

"Probably Buck wouldn't let her," Rose answered darkly.

As she walked up to the Ansel farmhouse, Rose saw that the yard was untidy. Weeds grew everywhere.

Evidently Ellie had tried to plant a few violets near the farmhouse door, but they looked dried and dead.

Rose knocked.

"Don't you want me to come in with you?" Bitter Creek called to her.

"I hear someone coming," Rose called back. "If I need you, I'll let you know."

The door opened slowly and Rose could only stare at the figure standing in the doorway.

It was Ellie—but what a changed Ellie!

She was but a forlorn apparition of her former self.

Her once-lovely hair was dowdy and faded; her once-sparkling blue eyes were dim and red-rimmed from weeping.

There was a red mark blazing across one cheek and a black-and-blue bruise streaking across her forehead.

"Ellie," Rose cried, grabbing her and kissing her.

She felt Ellie's slender body cringe beneath her touch.

"Oh, Rose, I'm so glad to see you," Ellie cried and began to weep bitterly.

"We were worried when you didn't come to Rebecca's wedding," Rose explained.

"Oh, I couldn't come; not when I look like this," she moaned.

"What happened to you?" Rose asked and went quickly to the door to motion for Bitter Creek to come in.

Kate came in with him and they both gasped when they saw Ellie.

"Was it Buck? Did Buck do this to you?" Rose asked.

Before she could answer, they heard a whimper that came from a pallet so Bitter Creek went to investigate the broken pitiful sound.

"It's a boy, and he's all beaten up," he said slowly.

"Buck beat him for forgetting to shut the pasture gate. Almost killed him. I tried to stop him," Ellie explained.

"Give me some grease," Bitter Creek said.

Ellie moaned, "I can't stand up to him. He's awful mean when he gets mad. You tried to warn me, Rose, and I wouldn't listen. I wouldn't listen."

Bitter Creek took the proffered grease from Ellie and gently rubbed it into the boy's lash marks.

"He takes pleasure in beating the boys," Ellie went on. "I try to protect them and then he beats me, too."

"Oh, my poor dear Ellie," Rose murmured.

They heard a loud shout from the back yard.

It was Buck and he was roaring, "Tell that damned boy to get himself out here and get his chores done."

Link made an effort to get up, but sank back on the bed, groaning.

"Stay there, lad," Bitter Creek said kindly to the boy; and to Ellie, who had started to cry, he said, "I'll take care of this."

"Be careful," Rose cautioned.

She thought this was all a dream, a horrible nightmare—the welt-mutilated boy on the pallet, and Ellie bruised and beaten!

Kate, who had said nothing, now spoke. "For shame! Why didn't you take a shotgun and kill the brute?"

Ellie whispered, "I'm so afraid of him."

Rose and Kate went to the door to watch.

They saw Buck swaggering toward Bitter Creek.

"Get off my place," Buck growled.

Bitter Creek spoke pleasantly. "We came to see why you and Ellie didn't come to Rebecca's wedding."

"Foolishness," the man rasped. "We ain't got no time for such foolishness."

"It was a fine wedding," Bitter Creek went on cordially, "and we missed you."

"Get the hell off my place," Buck shouted. Then he yelled toward the house, "Hey, woman, I said for you to send that bastard, Link, out here."

Bitter Creek looked behind the man now and saw Hank cowering behind a tree nearby.

"Link is in no condition to come out here," Bitter Creek said quietly. "You evidently tried to kill him."

"Mind your own business," Buck barked. "He's mine, ain't he? I can kill him if I want to."

"There's a law against murder," Bitter Creek said quietly.

"Woman," the man cried again, "are you going to send that bastard out or am I going to have to drag him out and give you both a real taste of the leather?"

He went toward the house now, taking off his belt as he walked.

"You're a great one for hurting the helpless," Bitter Creek injected. "How about picking on someone your own size for a change?"

Buck looked startled for a moment, before he threw back his massive head and laughed. Then he lunged at Bitter Creek, who lithely side-stepped the huge and clumsy man.

Buck cursed and rushed toward Bitter Creek.

Again, Bitter Creek side-stepped him.

Buck was livid with rage now and picked up an ax that was lying on the ground nearby. He threw it with all his might.

Bitter Creek ducked.

Now it was Bitter Creek's turn. He advanced quietly toward the raging man and tackled the brute, who fell backward hitting his head on a rock that served as a step to a dilapidated shed. Blood seeped from Buck's head.

When Hank saw his father's condition he left his hiding place and fled toward the house.

Buck Ansel was dead. There was no investigation of his death. Everyone was relieved that he was gone.

"I'm with child," Ellie told Rose some days later.

"I can get tansy root for you," Rose offered.

"No, I want this baby. I can teach it to love instead of to hate and be cruel as Buck did."

"But you can't stay here alone with just Link and Hank," Rose pointed out.

"I sent a message to Rebecca and Bill inviting them to come here to live and they liked the idea. We'll be a happy, loving family."

"It's all worked out so beautifully," Rose cried happily to Bitter Creek later.

"Yes, now you are free of your family. From here on it's just you and me," he answered.

"I love you," she whispered. "I love you."

Chapter 13

Everyone loved Kate Meadows. She was so jolly, so likeable, that it was impossible not to feel great affection for her. Bill Doolin's men adored her. Rose loved her, too, and although Kate still presented a magnificent appearance, she regarded her as a mother figure. Goldish-white curls, piled high, framed Kate's doll-like face on which the skin, webbed with fine lines, was covered with a white powder.

Her soft girlish chin was infinitely lined, too, but her lips resembled the petals of a rose. And her eyes, perhaps her most outstanding feature, were a brilliant blue and spaced widely apart.

Kate believed in taking time to rest every day after the noon meal, so one day as Kate and Rose sat in the hotel dining room, Rose asked her, "You were the Queen of the Barbary Coast?"

She had asked this question often before and had always been enchanted with the answer, usually a different version of Kate's adventures.

"There's a time for sitting and a time for working," Kate declared, hoisting her heavy self away from the table and going to a corner of the dining room where there was a comfortable settee. She liked to carry on prolonged conversations in comfort.

Kate always talked with the air of a woman used to being admired. Whenever men were present, she would smile her brilliant smile and her big eyes would sparkle. And she always dressed in a loose sort of garment made of Turkish gauze heavily worked in colored wools. Invariably there were artificial red roses dangling someplace on her dress.

Today, as she settled herself on the settee with Rose beside her, she complimented the younger woman.

"You are a beautiful girl, Rose Dunn."

"Thank you." Rose smiled.

"And you have your whole life before you. Now that you are free of that family of yours, what do you intend to do?"

"Do?" Rose asked, taken aback.

"You don't intend to stay here and work for me forever, do you?" she queried. Then she hurried on to add, "Not that I don't want you, darlin'. I do. It's just I'm thinkin' of your future."

"I like it here. I'm satisfied to stay here forever."

"Holy devil, child," Kate exclaimed. "There's a great big beautiful world out there."

"I never want to leave you," Rose said stubbornly.

Kate laughed, pleased.

"Well, we'll see. I'll bet if that man of yours, handsome Bitter Creek, decided to take off for Mexico you would be right beside him."

"Mexico!" Rose cried, startled. "He hasn't said anything about going to Mexico, has he?"

"No, of course not." Kate laughed. "I love you, Rose Dunn. And I want you to stay here with me as long as you want to. It's just I don't want to see you get set in your ways and just want to set."

"I won't," Rose promised. "Now tell me about the Barbary Coast."

"Whoa," Kate protested. "One step at a time. You see, I was a young one living in a little town in Wisconsin on the shores of Lake Winnebago where there were acres of white pine."

Others had joined Kate and Rose now and Kate gave them a welcoming smile. She loved a group of listeners around her.

"It was a roaring frontier boom town," she went on, "and served as headquarters for a brawling pack of lumber barons. I tell you that little old town literally roared with the cutting of all that timber."

"Sounds exciting," someone put in.

"It was more than exciting," Kate rambled on. "There was always some kind of struggle going on between the barons for control of the timber. One time I remember one of the barons got up an army of two hundred hobnailed men who cut loose the rival companies' booms so as to open up their storage ponds and send the timber tumbling down the spring flood of the Mississippi."

"And then?" Rose urged, her green eyes sparkling with excitement.

"Well, then there were always lots of fires due to the pine slabs and sawdust drifting around," she went on, "and one day, I remember—it was on April twenty-eighth—there was a terrible fire. It was windy and someone came barreling down Main Street yelling that there was a fire at Anderson's Mill. Everything in the town, of course, was built of wood and the fire raced from the freight yard to the Opera House."

Kate was silent a few moments, remembering.

"But, time went on and I was growing up. I became the prettiest girl in town with my long blond curls and my blue eyes and my good figure. And I was the town flirt. Everyone said I was a 'little too fast' but I loved being the talk of the town."

"I'll bet you looked like a big wax doll," Rose put in.

"That I did." Kate giggled. "And then my mamma made me a red velvet skating dress. She thought I was about the cutest thing in the world. She made it with a circular skirt so it flared out when I skated. That shocked the church sewing circle no end!"

Everyone laughed.

"There was a figure-skating contest that winter and I entered. I think the whole town turned out. There I was with the sunlight touching the gold of my hair that peeped out from the little fur tippet of a hat that Mamma had made me, and I had my hands tucked demurely into a mink muff. Oh, I was a sight as I twirled and swooped through my figures. I knew what a fetching picture I made. I had studied myself for hours in the pier-glass mirror at home."

"And then what happened?" Rose asked eagerly.

"I knew the ladies in the audience were watching in outrage and their menfolk were watching with relish, but when I skimmed over the ice in front of the judges' platform, I saw the happy smiles on their faces. They announced, 'First prize goes to Miss Kate Andrews.' That was my name then. Well, I skated out to receive my blue ribbon and a box of candy!"

You were the belle of the ice pond," Rose cried in admiration and everyone laughed.

Yes, I was the belle of the ball," Kate exulted, "and I won not only that blue ribbon and a box of chocolates, but I won the heart of the town banker's son, Henry Wilkerson by name."

"You married him?" Rose exclaimed.

"Yes, and later I wished I hadn't," Kate said sadly. "But that's another story. I'll tell you that chapter tomorrow. It's time to get to work now."

That evening Rose asked Bitter Creek if Kate had really been the Queen of the Barbary Coast.

His reply was quick. "Not only Queen of the Barbary Coast but the Toast of the West Coast and the Queen of every man's heart."

"Were you in love with Kate?" Rose asked jealously.

"Honey, every man, old and young, falls in love with Kate."

"She said something about me leaving here someday. She said she didn't expect me to stay here and work for her forever."

"Honey, she didn't mean it that way. She meant for you to do some living. She wants you to get out

86

in the world and see it and live like she did."

Rose was indignant. "Well, I don't see that she's got so much to show for running all over the country."

"Honey, she's got the most precious thing in the world, and that is memories," he said sincerely. "And she's got hundreds of friends."

"Do you love me, Bitter Creek?" she asked wistfully.

"I love you more than life itself," he declared fervently.

Chapter 14

The next day, Rose leaned forward eagerly as Kate resumed her story.

"Everyone considered Henry Wilkerson a real catch. Well, I never did anything by halves and I fell badly in love with him. He wasn't really handsome, but he was very polite."

Her audience laughed at this description.

"What really impressed me, though, was the fact that his father owned some Colorado mining property. I thought we would be rich!"

She paused a moment and then added wistfully, "I always dreamed of being rich."

"I'll bet you were a beautiful bride," Rose put in.

"Yes, the wedding was a big success. I was a beautiful bride in the white dress Mamma made me and I carried roses. After the wedding, with Henry's father as a chaperone, we left for Colorado.

"Chaperone?" Rose echoed.

"We had no money and I found out Mr. Wilkerson did not have much either. The bank hadn't been too prosperous because of all the fires and the businesses being burned out."

She was silent a moment, then proceeded.

"I'll never forget the day we arrived. The train that bore us toward James Peal Mountain puffed along in a steep canyon beside the gushing waters of Clear Creek, a creek that was greenish gray because of the tailings from the mills."

"Wish I could have been there," a listener put in enthusiastically.

"Wish I could live it all over again," Kate said wistfully. "There was a lot of turmoil and noise and excitement and I was caught up in the boisterous activity. Everything was rough and tough and I loved it!"

"Did Henry like it, too?" someone asked.

"Henry? Hell, no. Henry was wishing he was back home, but I loved it. We got off the train at Blackhawk and caught the stage for a one-mile ride up to Gregory Gulch. We saw the miners scuffing along in the dusty road in their heavy boots; they were swinging lunch pails and singing a haunting sweet melody as they walked."

"Did Henry's father like it as much as you did, Kate?" someone else asked curiously.

"Sure did." Kate answered promptly. "I guess Henry's pa and me would have made a better pair than Henry and me. Well, our stage driver was a mighty interesting fellow and he told us all about the singers and their songs. Said they were Cornish songs and the miners were Cousin Jacks. That's why there was so much good stonework in the buildings."

"Sure would like to go there," Angelica, the laundress, put in while Kate paused in the telling

89

of her story to look around at the group before starting one of her regular lectures, the gist of which was always that anyone could do anything he or she wanted to do and could be any kind of person he or she chose.

The group listened to her respectfully and, the lecture over, Kate proceeded with her story.

"That stage driver told us that an opera house was going to be built before long. Well, then I got real excited. I'd always wanted to be on the stage and I thought this was my opportunity. Guess I began to suspect that Henry wasn't going to be too ambitious when it came to digging out ore."

"I'll bet you could have been a famous stage star," Maggie, one of the cooks, put in now.

"Well, I could see myself singing in an opera house all right. I was ready."

"Did you dance on the stage, too?" Angelica asked.

"Not just then. But, I liked what I saw. Blackhawk, Mountain City, Central City, Dogtown, and Nevadaville were all huddled on top of each other in the narrow bottom of stark treeless gulches in a sort of jigsaw fashion. There were mines, ore dumps, mills, shaft houses, blacksmith shops, livery stables, railroad trestles, cottages, and fine residences perched at crazy angles, some on stilts."

"Sounds interesting," a male listener put in.

"That it was," Kate agreed. "Nevada Gulch Saloon was shaped like a slice of pie because of the slant from which Spring met Nevada Gulch Street."

There was a shuffle of many feet at the door and the group looked up to see the cowboys from the Bar Q Ranch.

"Old Man Wuerst gave us the day off," they informed a delighted Kate. "Came in to eat and dance and drink."

"Welcome, welcome, boys," Kate shrieked.

"And that," Rose told Bitter Creek that evening, "was the end of the story hour."

Bitter Creek laughed. "You really sound disappointed."

"Oh, I could listen to Kate talk forever. She makes life sound so interesting."

"And that is how she wants your life to be, my darling," Bitter Creek said. "She wants you to live life to the fullest."

"But I am living life to the fullest," she answered quickly. "I have everything I want. I have you and I have Kate and I love working here. And there are the dances at night and there's always excitement and—"

"But it's other people's excitement, sweetheart," he explained. "Kate wants you to be in the center of the excitement."

"I guess I know what you mean," Rose answered, slowly, dubiously. "But for right now, I'm satisfied. This is a sort of peaceful, happy time for me. Now that I know Ellie and Rebecca are fine, I just want to love you and take things easy for a while."

He kissed her.

Chapter 15

The boys of the Bar Q Ranch had enjoyed their night at the hotel, a night to let off steam. After a hearty breakfast they were on their way back to the ranch.

Kate cheered them on with cries of "Hurry back, my buddies. You're always welcome."

Then she gathered her audience around her again and proceeded with her story. "After a noonday meal at the Teller House, Pa Wilkerson took Henry and me on a tour of inspection. We picked up Pa's two-seater buggy at a blacksmith shop where the brake had just been repaired and then set out for the Fourth of July mine out near Dogtown on Quartz Hill. It was really just a big hole in the ground."

"How do you remember all the things that happened?" a listener put in.

"Once-in-a-lifetime remembrances are never forgotten," Kate assured them. "Well, Pa Wilkerson explained that he intended to drive a shaft down two hundred feet deeper and it would be timbered. He hoped to find a profitable vein of quartz by that operation."

"And then?" prompted Rose.

"Well, this was the good part. Pa Wilkerson wanted Henry to work the mine in return for a large share of the profits. If Henry made good, the mine would be ours. But," — Kate stopped talking and heaved a big sigh — "Henry was no miner and would never be a miner. In fact, Henry was lazy."

"What happened then?" a voice spoke up.

"All that winter, Henry did nothing but play the big grand piano that stood in the lobby of the Teller House. The music made a soulful accompaniment to his singing of 'Home Sweet Home.' "

Everyone laughed.

"I realized our money was dwindling away fast and something had to be done fast. I moved us out of the Teller House and into a cottage on Spring Street. Henry didn't care. He spent his days mooning around at me. Finally I got him to employ a crew of Cornishmen to start driving the shaft at the Fourth of July mine. It was exciting. The heavy ore wagons trundled along and from surrounding hillsides one could hear the steady beat of pumps and the shriek of steam hoists. The narrow-gauge railway at Blackhawk was hauling in machinery for mine shafts and for the stamping mills."

"Sounds exciting," said Bitter Creek, who came into the dining room now.

"Oh, it is exciting," Rose cried. "Come, sit down and listen."

Bitter Creek winked at Kate and sat near Rose.

"Then we got the bad news. The assayer's report said our vein was no good. In fact the samples of ore taken from the Fourth of July weren't even worth testing. Henry wanted to quit and go back home, but I am no quitter. I put on old clothes and tucked my golden curls under a cap and went down into that shaft."

"Hurrah for you!" Bitter Creek applauded.

Kate blew him a kiss and resumed her tale. "By this time, I realized that my husband, Henry P. Wilkerson, was no go-getter and I was ready to call it quits. Besides, a certain gentleman called Stony Brown had entered my life, so we went to San Francisco. But that is another story."

"I want to ask you a question, Kate," Angelica asked. "Why did Mr. Wilkerson call the mine the Fourth of July mine?"

"That's an easy question to answer. That Pa Wilkerson was the most patriotic man I ever saw. He loved his country far more than he loved that son of his. I guess if Henry and me would have had a baby he would have wanted to call it America."

Chapter 16

In her room at the Ingalls Hotel that night, snuggled in Bitter Creek's arms, Rose sighed contentedly.

"I'm so happy," she murmured.

"Wouldn't you like to have some excitement in your life, Rose?" Bitter Creek asked.

"No," Rose answered quickly. "I like my life just the way it is. I love the dances and I love Kate and I love helping Kate run the hotel and most of all I love you."

"I love you, too," he whispered.

Presently, he spoke out of the silence. "America Wilkerson. America Newcomb."

Rose laughed. "You're teasing me. America Newcomb!"

He was very serious when he spoke again. "No, there can never be an America Newcomb."

"Why not?"

"Because she would be a bastard," he said matter-of-factly. "You won't marry me."

"Oh, darling, don't start that again. I can't marry you. The very word 'marriage' makes me sick. Let's just go along the way we are. We love each other."

"That we do," he assured her.

Rose liked Bill Doolin and was intrigued by his colorful past.

"Bill and I have been friends for a long time," Bitter Creek told her. "We trust each other. I first met Bill—believe I've told you this before—when we both worked for O.D. Halsell at the H X Ranch on the Cimarron. Bill and I were just young'uns when we first met. Bill was a tall, lanky Arkansas boy who knew how to use an ax and build corrals and sheds."

"Didn't he leave the HX Ranch?"

"Yes, Bill decided he wanted some excitement. He rode off and joined up with the Daltons. He was in on the Red Rock train robbery when the Dalton gang robbed two trains at once. After the Coffeyville massacre, he organized his own gang. That's when I joined up with him."

"Would you ever like to settle down, Bitter Creek?" Rose asked now wistfully. "Would you like to get a farm and raise cattle?"

"And an America Newcomb?" he questioned.

"Your teasing me again," she whispered.

"Yes, Rose, sometime I think it might be right nice not to have to look over my shoulder all the time, not to have to be afraid every time I go to bed."

"You aren't afraid here with me?" she asked.

"No, of course not. But when I hear a board creak, or a branch snap, I think the law is closing in. Even when I go out to the pump to draw a bucket of water, I wonder if someone will shoot me in the back."

"Poor Bitter Creek," Rose said softly, kissing him.

"You make it all worthwhile," he murmured. "You're my woman."

"You haven't seen a woman that you wanted since we met?" she questioned.

"No, all women look alike to me now. There's no woman except you that is rounded and sweet and has green eyes and beautiful hair."

"I worry about you, sweetheart," she said presently. "I worry for fear something might happen to you."

"We have to take the bitter with the sweet," he murmured. "We must take just one day at a time and enjoy each moment."

"Kate asked me the other day if it was true that I jumped out of the window into your arms when you and I left the old farmhouse where Pa lived," she related.

Bitter Creek laughed merrily. "That's the way I thought it would be. I thought I would rescue you from your mean old pa. I heard that story before. I think Red Buck drinks too much whiskey and dreams up these fables."

"I like Red Buck, even though he has a wild imagination and dreams up all kinds of stories," she conceded.

"He means well," Bitter Creek said and fell to nibbling her ear and then her breasts, first one and then the other.

A few days later, they had a surprise visitor. Bill Eckridge rode into town with the startling news that he had heard that Bree had taken a sudden interest in the voluptuous, red-headed Mary Kahns!

Rose could hardly believe her ears.

"That can't be," she cried. "Bree called her a whore."

"Well, from what I hear things have changed. Bree even feels sorry for that mean Ira."

"Does Pa know?"

"Sure he knows, and he's as mean about it as a mad bull. He's rantin' and ravin' all over the place."

"Maybe Bree has just found out how to get to Pa. Maybe he's found he can really make him mad by pretending to be interested in Mary," Rose mused.

"I don't know," Bill said slowly. He was obviously embarrassed. "I don't know."

Bitter Creek and Rose laughed about it afterward.

"Imagine Pa and Bree both after that fat Mary Kahns?"

"She does have her charms," Bitter Creek joked.

"What charms?"

"Red hair, a big bosom, and galloping hips."

"Would her charms appeal to you, Bitter Creek?" Rose asked.

"The only charms that appeal to me are green eyes, a peaches-and-cream complexion, and fluttering lashes like butterfly wings," he said.

"Oh, Bitter Creek, I love you."

"What's come over Bill Doolin?" Kate asked

Bitter Creek one evening.

"He's the same old Bill as far as I can see," Bitter Creek said.

"No, he's acting mighty different. He's sitting around and staring into space."

"Maybe he's in love," Rose offered.

"Bill Doolin in love!" Bitter Creek snorted. "Bill loves them all. There's Emma and Candy and Evelyn and Bertha and—"

Kate laughed. "I know Bill Doolin and that man will never fall in love. Not like you and Bitter Creek are in love," she said to Rose. "He's all wrapped up in planning robberies and having a good time. And don't forget the poker table."

"Maybe he's planning another big job," Rose put in hopefully.

"I don't know, but I do know that he ain't acting like himself," Kate said definitely.

There was a dance that evening and many people dropped in at the hotel. Some of them were strangers just passing through, but Doolin and Bitter Creek and Kate made everyone welcome; the gang was used to people coming to the hotel for the dances.

But on this particular evening, two young girls arrived who were obviously very much out of place. They were poorly clad and dirty. Even Red Buck, who was never very particular in his choice of dancing partners, turned his nose up at this pair.

"Where you girls from?" Kate asked curiously.

"We're from out that way." The one pointed

over her shoulder.

"And your name?" Kate inquired.

"I'm known as Cattle Annie and this is my partner, Little Britches," the girl said seriously.

"And how old might you be?" Kate asked politely.

"I'm all of sixteen years old and she's about fifteen," the girl answered.

"Don't you think you're a bit young to be comin' to a place like this?"

"It's just a dance, ain't it?" the girl asked. "We heard the Doolin gang was here and we were a mite curious to see the famous Doolin gang."

Kate laughed and began to point out the various members of the gang.

The girls' eyes popped out with excitement.

"And who is that varmint over there?" Little Britches asked.

"That is an hombre known as Rattlesnake." Kate laughed. "I'll bet you would really like him."

"How about making my acquaintance with him?"

This Kate did and she laughed as the two she had just introduced began to jiggle up and down in a sort of dance.

"I guess you would like a partner, too," she told Cattle Annie.

"I like that one," she said pointing to Red Buck.

"That's Red Buck," Kate answered. "You're a bit young for him.

"He's a mighty good-looking man. I like his red hair," she complimented.

"Yes, Red Buck is a good-looking man, but this

one named Sawdust is more your type," she said. "Hey, Sawdust," she called to the outlaw in question. "Want you to meet Cattle Annie."

When the dance was over, Cattle Annie and Little Britches promised to attend the next dance.

"What a pair!" Kate sighed as she watched the two ride off on a sorry-looking mule.

Chapter 17

Cattle Annie and Little Britches were back the next evening.

This time, they had clean faces and clean hands.

Rattlesnake and Sawdust, suddenly in the limelight because of their association with the strange new creatures, appeared to enjoy their company.

Rattlesnake presently gave Little Britches a token of his esteem. It was a piece of a leather belt. She acted as though he had given her a piece of gold.

While Doolin sawed away at his fiddle, the other dancers enjoyed the comical sight of Cattle Annie and Little Britches jumping up and down with their partners, Rattlesnake and Sawdust.

As time went by Sawdust declared his love for Cattle Annie, whose real named turned out to be Annie McDougal. So one night, the energetic Annie stole the clothes of a hired man on her father's farm and rode off into the sunset with her outlaw lover. But as she galloped along, she lost control of her horse and she was thrown. This so disgusted her lover, Sawdust, that he deserted her and she was forced to walk ten miles across the prairie to her home.

The next day, Sawdust appeared at her door and humiliated her further by telling her he did not love her, had never loved her, and could never love a woman who could not sit a horse!

Heartsick but determined, she persuaded Little Britches, whose real name was Jennie Stevens, to run away and join the Doolin gang. Together, the girls trailed the gang to their hide-out at Old Rock Fort on Deer Creek in Oklahoma. There, the girls became the servants of the Doolin gang. They delivered their messages, stole horses, and watched the roads, and acted as a sort of comedy-relief team.

On a beautiful evening in July, Bill Doolin led the gang into Cimarron, Kansas, where they robbed the Cimarron National Bank of several thousand dollars. But as Doolin and the gang left the bank and started down the main street, townspeople, hiding behind fences and trees, opened fire. Bill Doolin went down with a bullet in his leg; Bitter Creek helped him mount his horse, and with six-shooters blazing, they thundered out of town.

The telegraph clicked out the news. Posses formed and chased the gang to the border.

Bill Doolin still managed to lead his men to safety. Bill and Bitter Creek went to a ranch in the Cheyenne and the gang went to the hide-out at Old Fort Rock.

At the ranch in the Cheyenne, Bill Doolin nursed his wound and plotted the next job. He also told Bitter Creek that for the first time in his life he had a desire to settle down.

Bitter Creek could hardly believe his ears. Bill

Doolin was a wanderer who loved his freedom. He loved women and poker and taking wild chances when robbing a train or bank. To think of him wanting to settle down startled Bitter Creek.

"Do you have someone in mind you would like to settle down with, Bill?" Bitter Creek asked.

"Yes."

Chapter 18

Bitter Creek told Rose about it later.

"Out of a clear blue sky," Bitter Creek related their conversation, "Bill says he's thinking of settling down."

Rose laughed.

"Bill Doolin will never settle down," she said later when Bitter Creek told her that Bill had admitted he had a woman in mind.

"Have you met her?" Rose asked curiously. "Is she one of the saloon girls?"

"Hell, no. Bill would never settle down with a saloon queenie. Not Bill."

"But you are with him most of the time. Who could it be?"

The days went by and Bill said nothing more. One day, Bitter Creek broached the subject. "Sometime back, you said something about settling down, Bill. Thought any more about it?"

"That's all I think about," Bill admitted. "I think about it night and day. I don't even have any heart anymore about planning a job."

Summer came and the land smoldered under a blazing sun.

The gang had gathered in Ingalls. Doolin ruled them with iron discipline, and although they whiled away their days playing poker, joking, and drinking as soon as Bill had the next job planned, they would be ready to strike.

Meanwhile, the long hot summer days went by.

One of the gang was always riding out of Ingalls to meet Cattle Annie or Little Britches for news of the law that seemed always to be on their trail.

In August, a stranger appeared in Ingalls. He said his name was Bloody Turner. He had blazing red hair and a ready smile and he was a good poker player.

When Rose met the newcomer, she felt uneasy.

"There's something about him," she told Bitter Creek, "that I don't like. I don't trust him."

Bitter Creek laughed. "He can't do no harm. He's a damned good poker player. He'll drift on one of these days."

And drift on he did, but Rose was so positive that he was a lawman, that she eventually convinced Bitter Creek of that fact.

"Why don't we move on?" she asked Bitter Creek one day.

"Move on?"

"Let's go down Texas way, Bitter Creek," she begged. "We can make a whole new start. No one will know you."

"You sound like you would like to settle down. You sound like Bill Doolin!"

"Don't laugh at me," Rose cried. "I'm really serious. For the first time I feel that the law is closing in."

Bitter Creek relayed her fears to Bill Doolin and both men laughed.

"Bill wants you and me to go with him come Sunday," Bitter Creek informed Rose one day as she was busy at the hotel.

"Where to?"

"To church," Bitter Creek replied, grinning.

"Bill Doolin intends to go to church!" Rose exclaimed. "I can't believe it."

"It's true. It's a little church way over by Bittersweet Creek. There's going to be a box social, so fix up a box for me to bid on."

"I'll fix up a box like the one you bought that first Sunday I laid eyes on you," she vowed, dimpling. "I'll have to put goldenrod on it instead of daisies though. It's too late in the year for daisies."

"Is he going to bid on someone's box?" Rose asked.

"You know as much about it as I do," Bitter Creek said. "All I know is he wants us to go with him to a box social."

Chapter 19

It seemed to Rose that the months had rolled back and this was the first day she had set eyes on Bitter Creek. The church was much the same — a small log cabin set in the woods. The congregation was fluttering about; the women with boxes in their hands, the men anxious for the bidding to begin.

The minute Rose and Bitter Creek saw Edith Ellsworth, they knew she was the object of Bill Doolin's eye. She was a beauty. She looked like an angel with her soft, shining blond hair, her clear blue eyes, her skin as soft as the petal of a white rose.

Bill said simply, "This is my wife-to-be, Edith."

And just looking at them together, Rose knew that Edith Ellsworth and Bill Doolin loved each other.

Edith was a minister's daughter.

Rose could not help but wonder if the Rev. Emil Ellsworth knew that his daughter was in love with a notorious outlaw. Yet, Bill Doolin could be gentle and kind and compassionate, and looking at him now as he smiled at Edith she knew that Edith could trust her life to Bill.

As Bill and Bitter Creek and Rose rode back from Lawton to Ingalls, Bill told them of his plans.

He intended to be married by Edith's minister father.

"Does he know who you are?" Rose asked.

"No, he thinks I am a cattle buyer," Bill said crisply.

"Does Edith know?" This from Bitter Creek.

"Yes. I told her all about myself and the gang and that there is a price of six thousand dollars on my head. She understands."

"Oh, Bill," Rose moaned putting her hands on his.

They rode along in silence for a long while and presently Rose spoke. "Why don't we four go to Texas?"

The two men looked at her as if she were crazy. She said nothing more.

Edith Ellsworth and William Doolin were married in early winter in the parlor of her father, the Rev. Emil Ellsworth.

Mrs. Minnie Ellsworth looked worried and sad and Rose surmised that she knew of the occupation of her daughter's husband-to-be.

As for Edith, she was radiant with happiness. Gowned in a simple white dress and with a white satin ribbon tucked in her blond curls, Rose thought she looked more like an angel than ever. There was something ethereal about her, something unearthly.

Bill Doolin was gazing at her as though he could not believe his good fortune in winning her love.

Rose, in a simple pink gown with a pink satin ribbon in her hair, stood next to Edith; and Bitter Creek, in his Sunday-best, stood next to Bill Doolin as his best man.

The wedding ceremony began.

Bill Doolin took Edith's frail white hand in his and held it lovingly.

"Repeat after me," the minister intoned. "I, William Doolin, take thee, Edith Ellsworth, to my wedded wife."

Bill repeated the words, softly, lovingly.

The minister went on. "To have and to hold from this day forward."

Bill repeated the words.

"For better, for worse," the minister continued, "for richer, for poorer, in sickness and in health."

Bill repeated the words and added, "Forever, my darling."

Rev. Ellsworth cleared his throat and continued, "To love and to cherish, till death us do part, according to God's holy ordinance."

Bill said the words slowly.

Rose looked at Bitter Creek and saw that he was staring at her. She could almost read his mind. He was thinking, "Isn't this beautiful? You and I should get married."

She jerked her gaze away from his as the minister continued, "And thereto I plight thee my troth."

Bill breathed the words, softly, carefully, and then it was Edith's turn.

She repeated each word slowly, looking straight into Bill's eyes as she talked.

When her father concluded that part of the ceremony with Edith's words, "I give thee my troth," Rose stifled an impulse to cry.

Rev. Ellsworth was speaking to the groom now. "Wilt thou have this woman to thy wedded wife, to live together after God's ordinance in the holy estate of matrimony? Wilt thou love her, comfort her, honor and keep her in sickness and in health; and, forsaking all others, keep thee only unto her, as long as ye both shall live?"

Bill Doolin spoke sincerely when he answered, "I will."

The minister spoke now to his daughter. "Wilt thou have this man to thy wedded husband, to live together after God's ordinance in the holy estate of matrimony? Wilt thou love him, comfort him, honor and keep him in sickness and in health; and, forsaking all others, keep thee only unto him, as long as ye both shall live?"

Edith's answer was fervent. "I will."

And it was over. Bill Doolin, outlaw, and Edith Ellsworth, a young woman with the face of an angel, were married.

Rose had supposed that Bill would take rooms at Kate's hotel for Edith and himself. But not so. He rented a white frame house on the edge of town.

Rose was rather affronted by this action.

"It's as though he thinks she's too good to board here at Kate's. I suppose she won't be coming to the dances either."

"I doubt it."

"She thinks she's too good to come to the dances?"

"Of course not. But Rose, you have to realize that they are on their honeymoon. They want to be alone."

"Alone?"

"You have to realize, too, Rose, that Bill has put his Edith up on a pedestal. He worships that woman. He calls her his gem."

"And what do you call me?" she teased, dimpling at him.

"You are my darling," he answered promptly.

"But you don't care if I dance with Buck and Sawdust and all the rest of them?"

"Of course not. I want you to have a good time." He laughed.

"I love to go to the dances and I love to see those two funny girls, Cattle Annie and Little Britches, jumping around like two jumping jacks."

"As long as you have a good time, I'm happy only—" He stopped talking to gaze sadly at her.

"Only what?"

"I want to marry you and I would like for us to have a white house like Bill and Edith."

She turned sadly away.

Later she told him she was sorry. "I can't help feeling the way I feel. If we were married, I would feel like I was poor old Ma having to endure what she had to endure from Pa."

"You talk crazy," he said mildly.

"Maybe I'll feel differently after a while."

"Maybe," he said wearily, turning away.

Chapter 20

Spring came to Ingalls, Oklahoma, that year in great magic strides, not softly or shyly. It spread its glory in the flush of green on the poplar trees, the elms, and the oaks. It's radiance filled the air that was scented with the fragrance of violets and anemones.

And with spring Daniel Dunn came home from the gold fields where he had had a bit of luck. He came back to buy a farm, but he went directly to the hotel to see Rose.

He stared at her for a long moment because he had not seen her in her new finery.

She was overjoyed to see him and clung to him crying, "You've come home. Oh, Daniel, I'm so glad to see you."

When he spoke, it was to say icily, "I've heard about you. Don't you know they call you Bitter Creek's woman?"

"That's what I am," she said frankly.

"Bitter Creek Newcomb's woman!" He flung the words out. "They call you other things, too. You're a whore. Remember when Bree called Mary Kahns a whore? We were all shocked. Well, that's what you are. You are a whore!"

"Don't say that," she cried. "Don't ever say that. I'm not a whore. I love Bitter Creek and he loves me. He wants me to marry him, but I shrink at the word 'marriage.' You know how it was with Pa and Ma."

"That's no excuse," he shouted. "You are just taking the easy way out. It's easy to say something makes you do this or that."

"Oh, Daniel, I thought you would understand. You and I were always so much alike."

"I don't want my sister called a whore," he protested stubbornly.

"I'm trying to change my mind about marriage," she went on. "I truly am. Bitter Creek begs me to marry him."

"Then marry him and make an honest woman out of yourself," he instructed her coldly.

Seeking to change the subject, she asked, "Have you been out to the home place?"

"Thought I'd ride out there this afternoon and look around. Maybe Bree knows of a good farm for sale."

"You hit it rich?" she asked.

"No, just enough to buy a farm. I'm a farmer at heart, Rose. I got sick and tired of trying to get gold out of those hills. Everything was sky-high, everybody out trying to make a dollar. Can you believe eggs were seventy-five cents a dozen and a small potato cost twenty-five cents?"

Bitter Creek joined them then and welcomed Daniel with open arms.

Daniel felt much more relaxed with Bitter Creek so they went to the bar for a drink.

Rose pouted. Then she consoled herself with the knowledge that Daniel would be riding out to the home place and she would get a firsthand report of happenings at Pa's.

She could well imagine Mary flaunting her voluptuous figure around the old kitchen. She could almost see her swinging those big breasts over the breakfast table, as Ira, with his wicked little eyes, encouraged her on.

Bitter Creek returned presently to inform her that Daniel had started for the old farm. "Seems as though the trip to the gold fields did the boy good," he said. "Seems like a grown man now."

"He's bitter because we aren't married," she informed him.

"I know. He told me and I told him I would marry you this minute, but you won't marry me."

"I love you," she said softly.

"You think that by saying 'I love you,' you make everything right," he said turning away from her.

She went to him then and said, "Couldn't you and I go into the woods alone and say our marriage vows?"

"We could and I would like that, but it is not binding in the eyes of the law."

"What does the law mean to us anyway?" she asked practically. "We don't care anything about the law."

"I know, honey, but underneath I have a kind of respect for the law."

"That's a strange thing to say," she said lightly, but suddenly her voice trembled when she said, "I *do* love you, Bitter Creek, and I consider myself

Mrs. George Bitter Creek Newcomb."

Daniel returned that evening. He seemed to be bursting with news of events at the farm.

"Were they surprised to see you?" Rose asked as she and Bitter Creek took him to the dining room for supper.

He gulped his coffee down before taking up his story.

"They were plenty surprised to see me," he began. "Pa just looked at me with his eyes bulging out. Bree grabbed my hand and shook it and that half-witted Ira tried to pinch me."

"And Mary Kahns? What did Mary Kahns do?" This from Rose.

"That woman!" Daniel exclaimed. "She came strutting out to my horse and looked up at me and winked."

"Winked?" Rose cried, amazed, "Why would she wink?"

"Guess she thought she was makin' up to me," he said modestly. "Anyway she's as fat as ever. She had her red hair braided in a sort of crown around her head and it looked to me as if she had smeared red berries on her cheeks. She looked right fetching."

Bitter Creek laughed merrily at this. "That woman," he drawled, "couldn't look enticing if she had a silk scarf draped around her."

"Anyway," Daniel continued, "they all seemed right glad to see me. We went into the kitchen and Mary Kahns set a cup of coffee in front of me."

"I'll bet she dangled those big breasts of hers

116

right before your nose, too," Bitter Creek commented, chuckling.

Daniel blushed and ducked his head.

"I see those gold fields haven't changed you much, Daniel, my boy." Bitter Creek laughed. "And I'm glad to see you that way. It doesn't pay to get tough."

"Well, I'm not very tough, I guess," Daniel asserted now.

"Go on and tell us what happened next," Rose prodded.

"When I mentioned I had come back to settle down near here and was looking for a farm, Pa slapped me on the back and said I should put my money in the old farm and we could expand—"

"You wouldn't do that?" Rose breathed in disbelief. "You surely wouldn't do that, Daniel?"

"No, of course not," he said definitely. "I want no part of Pa and his farm. When Pa said this, Bree glared at me and I saw Mary Kahns give him a warning look."

"Do you think Mary likes Bree?" Rose could not resist asking the question.

"Yes, I do," Daniel faltered slowly. "I was going to watch out for signs that she liked Bree and I saw them. She kept giving him warning looks out of the sides of her eyes."

"After all, Bree is younger than Pa and he's going to be on this earth a longer time than Pa," Bitter Creek pointed out.

"I was almost ashamed to look for the signs," Daniel went on, "but I couldn't help noticing. Ira hung onto Bree, too. It seemed to me that Bree is now head of the house."

Rose spoke in a hushed tone. "Is the strop still hanging by the door?"

"No, it's gone," Daniel said. "That was one of the first things I noticed, that that damned strop was gone. Guess Bree took care of that."

"I still get scared just thinking about that strop," Rose observed.

"Many's the time I felt it bite into my skin," Daniel said bitterly.

"Well, that's all in the past now," Bitter Creek said cheerfully. "You've got the money for a farm and we're going to have the pleasure of your company off and on, I hope."

"Did anything else happen?" Rose asked.

"Well, when Pa saw that I wasn't going to put my money in the old farm, he got real cranky. He started cussing and carrying on. Both Bree and Mary Kahns just ignored him."

"Strange, we all call Mary Kahns by her full name," Rose mused.

"Just seems Mary isn't enough of a name for her," Daniel said, laughing.

Their suppers were served now and they were silent as they ate.

Presently, Rose asked, "You are going to stay here at the hotel, aren't you, Daniel until you find your farm?"

"Yes, I would like that. Bree told me of several good farms for sale and I'll go around and look at those."

"I've got a pretty good eye for the land, Daniel. I'll go with you when I can, to look," Bitter Creek offered.

Daniel smiled his thanks.

His parting words to her that night were, "I still want you and Bitter Creek to get married, Rose. Someday you may wish you had married him and it may be too late then."

Daniel's words lingered with her as she prepared to go to bed.

Bitter Creek was at Doolin's little white house; they were planning a job.

Rose felt suddenly lonely.

She resented Daniel's holier-than-thou attitude and she resented Bitter Creek's visits to Doolin's home.

She had never been invited to his love nest, as she called it.

She had expected an invitation, but Bitter Creek put her off with such excuses as, "Edith wants everything to be just perfect before she has company."

"But I'm not company," Rose protested. "I'm almost like her family."

"I know, darling," Bitter Creek comforted her. "Just be patient."

Well, she was tired of being patient. She wanted to visit the little white house. The way Bill Doolin and Bitter Creek acted about Edith was ridiculous, she thought. They expected everyone to treat her as though she was something precious.

She reminded herself that Bill Doolin did call his wife his gem.

Chapter 21

On a late spring day when Rose was helping Kate in the hotel, they had a visitor. Rose was at the registration desk and Kate was sitting nearby working on a ledger, but they both looked up at the same time to see a woman standing in the doorway. Rose noted that she was young and beautiful, but she was unprepared for Kate's cry, "Amaryllis."

"Mother," the young woman cried and they were in each other's arms.

Rose watched as Kate hugged and kissed the newcomer.

Then she tearfully introduced Rose to her daughter. "This is Amaryllis, my daughter," she said proudly.

"I didn't know you had a daughter," Rose blurted.

Amaryllis spoke up now. "Mother, I had to come. I needed you. I made Allen Spence tell me where you were. Oh, I appreciated the checks you sent every month for me to stay at the Alden School, but Mother, I needed you."

After Kate and Amaryllis left the lobby of the hotel, Rose sat wondering where this daughter had come from. She remembered Kate's joke about having to name her daughter America Wilkerson, but this definitely was no America Wilkerson.

Rose told Bitter Creek about the newcomer and he was as curious as she.

"Is she pretty?" he asked.

"Very,"· she answered frankly. "She's very blond. I think she must dip her hair."

"Well, I'm anxious to see her. Probably we'll get to know more about her this evening. Tonight's a big dance, too. Guess all the gang will be anxious to meet Kate's daughter."

Kate exhibited Amaryllis proudly at the evening meal in the dining room.

Amaryllis wore a dress of green satin with pink roses bunched cleverly at the neckline.

Rose, looking at her, knew that Amaryllis was no mere schoolgirl. She was a woman of the world. It showed plainly in the way she slithered those enormous blue eyes around and in the knowing twist to her petal-like lips.

Rose could study her at leisure now. She saw the pure gold of her hair, the rose-petal quality of her skin. She appreciated the shape of her face and her mouth that was just a hint wide. And she was impressed by her eyes, gentian blue with dark sweeping lashes.

To deny Amaryllis' beauty would be to deny the beauty of a full-blown rose or of a crimson sunrise.

Bitter Creek, on being introduced to Amaryllis said simply, "You are beautiful."

And she smiled at him, fully knowledgeable of the value of her petal-smooth skin, her gorgeous blue eyes.

"She's too pretty," Red Buck said huskily. "She can't be real."

Daniel was smitten as were most of the other men at the dance that evening.

Heretofore Rose had been the belle of the ball, sought after for dances. Now it was Amaryllis who was acting coy and sweet when the men stood in line to dance with her. And Rose was furious.

Bitter Creek tried to console her. "It's just that she's a new face, honey. All the fellows want to dance with her and make her feel welcome."

"Is she prettier than me?" Rose demanded.

"Of course not. As I told you, she's a new face, a new fresh face."

"So you think my face is old," Rose exploded angrily.

"Simmer down, honey," he cautioned. "You are making a scene. The boys will be around to ask you to dance."

"I don't care if they do or not," she shot back. "I'm going upstairs. Are you coming?"

"No, I want to stick around for the excitement. I've got a feeling there'll be some action around here tonight."

Feeling like an abandoned child, Rose went upstairs to her room.

Her world was falling apart, she realized. Daniel had come back to condemn her. Bitter Creek preferred to stay downstairs and watch the dazzling Amaryllis exercise her magic on Bill Doolin's gang.

It was obvious that Kate idolized this beautiful daughter of hers. No doubt, Amaryllis would help out in the hotel and assume Rose's place.

Rose cried herself to sleep.

Early the next morning, Rose went down to breakfast. Kate greeted her affectionately and asked why she hadn't stayed at the dance the evening before.

"I had a headache," she lied.

"The dances just aren't the same without you," Kate observed. "You add such a sparkle to everything."

"Did Amaryllis enjoy the dance?" Rose asked.

"Yes, but she isn't used to such strenuous dancing," Kate answered. "Her type of dancing is more on the dainty side."

Rose stifled her impulse to question this statement and kept her mouth shut.

"Is she still in bed?" Rose asked. "I thought we might have breakfast together."

"The dear is completely worn out. She had such a tiring journey. She intends to stay in bed until noon," Kate divulged.

A smiling, apologetic Amaryllis presently came into the dining room. She wore a poppy-splotched dress and had a crimson bow in her blond hair.

"I'm sorry, Mother," she cried, kissing Kate enthusiastically.

"No need to apologize," Kate assured her. "Rose is my helper."

Amaryllis scowled at Rose, who nodded a pleasant, "Good morning."

Bitter Creek came into the dining room and immediately Amaryllis' scowl vanished and she flashed her pearly teeth at him.

"And how is the lovely Miss Amaryllis this morning?" he greeted her cordially.

"Just fine, thank you." She smiled coyly. "And how is the most handsome man in Ingalls?"

"Are you, miss, referring to me?" he asked, but Rose could tell he was pleased at the flattery.

"I am, indeed."

She smiled again and moved closer to him, blinking her long lashes as she asked, "And where did you disappear to last evening? I especially wanted to dance with you."

"I would have liked that," he answered, "but I had a previous engagement."

Rose breathed a sigh of relief. He hadn't stayed at the dance after all. He had gone to the Doolins' as was his custom lately and had stayed all night in their spare room.

Amaryllis continued to smile at Bitter Creek.

"May I sit with you while you eat?" she asked him, then turned to her mother. "I'll have just a bit of breakfast."

Rose wanted to snap, "It's past time for serving breakfast."

"Of course," Kate was quick to respond. "You two just sit right down here and I'll have Augusta bring something out from the kitchen."

Rose stood there feeling like the hired help. How could Kate do this to her? She knew that she and Bitter Creek always ate together.

As the days went by, she realized that she had a very real rival in Amaryllis Meadows.

124

"Better marry him while you can," Daniel advised her. "It already may be too late."

"What do you mean too late?" she demanded.

"That Amaryllis is out to get him for her man."

"She couldn't get Bitter Creek away from me," Rose declared.

"I wouldn't bet on that," he went on. "I thought at first she was all softlike, all peaches and cream; but underneath all that beauty, she's as hard as nails."

"I thought that the first time I saw her," Rose said. "All this talk about her being an innocent schoolgirl is just talk! She's tough."

"I'm surprised Kate doesn't see through her," Daniel said.

"Me, too," Rose agreed. "But blood is thicker than water. She's crazy about Amaryllis."

"Well, if Bitter Creek still wants to marry you, better get him to the altar quick," Daniel advised.

He had found the farm he wanted to buy, just a few miles out of Ingalls. He invited Rose and Bitter Creek to come out to inspect the place before he put down the payment. Rose accepted the invitation, but Bitter Creek said he had a meeting with Doolin.

"Does he really have a meeting with Doolin?" Daniel asked as they rode off to the farm.

"Yes, they are planning a big job," Rose said. "Bitter Creek has never lied to me, but I know that he is flattered by Amaryllis paying so much attention to him."

"She's after him," Daniel said darkly.

"She's not going to get him," Rose promised.

"Then you'll have to get tough, too," he advised. "Go to that dance tonight and glitter."

"I will, I will," she cried. "And I'll be the belle of the ball."

At the dance that night, she swirled into the room. She had taken her party dress of red satin and lowered the neckline to show half her bosom.

Bitter Creek stared at her when he saw her and then whispered, "What are you trying to do?"

"I love you," she said simply, dimpling up at him.

"Holy devil!" he breathed.

Rose could not deny that he was smitten by Amaryllis' beauty and charm. It was hard to bear. But Rose could think of nothing else to do except to bear it—for now, anyway, until he came to his senses.

She was sure he was bewitched. He would say in an offhand manner, "Amaryllis was telling me about California today. You know she is really like a little girl."

"A little girl!" Rose would inject acidly. "A little girl! She's a witch."

"She doesn't realize how very beautiful she is," he went on, too absorbed in the thought of Amaryllis to have noticed what Rose said.

"I'm sure she dips her hair," Rose said.

Absorbed in his thoughts, he did not hear her. In fact, he hardly seemed to know she existed.

On afternoon, she saw Amaryllis standing on the veranda of the hotel twirling a large pink parasol slowly over her blond head.

Bitter Creek was smiling down at her and the two might have been in a world apart. They were oblivious of anyone who might be watching them.

Then she saw Amaryllis take Bitter Creek's proffered arm and walk down the wide main street of Ingalls.

It wasn't to be borne! It wasn't to be borne!

Amaryllis was flaunting her conquest of Bitter Creek before the whole town. It was bad enough the way she hung on to him at the dances, but in front of the whole town, it was unbearable!

Perhaps she had waited too long? Perhaps Bitter Creek wouldn't want to marry her now. Well, she intended to find out.

Chapter 22

Her plan to be belle of the ball had not entirely failed.

Dimpling, laughing, flirting with the gang had been a decided success. Amaryllis, seeing Rose's popularity, had relinquished the field to her and retreated with her captive, Bitter Creek.

"You're our favorite," Red Buck declared loudly and the gang took up the cry.

"That woman, Amaryllis, is an icicle," Arizona Tom declared.

"We like our women warm and loving," declared Little Bill.

"And we don't like anyone making fun of our little women, Cattle Annie and Little Britches," Tulsa Andrew shouted.

"Yeah, when Cattle Annie came in the other night to the dance to warn us about those deputies buzzing around, that Amaryllis made fun of her," Red Buck said angrily. "She ain't got no call to make fun of Cattle Annie or Little Britches. They belong to us."

Kate, overhearing their remarks, was quick to defend her daughter. "She just don't know anything about these things. She's been protected in that school out in California. I paid a lot of money to keep her in that school."

Some of the men rolled their eyes upward at these remarks.

"If that Amaryllis can pull the wool over her ma's eyes, she can do anything. I can see through that brazen hussy," Red Buck said.

Now that the gang had acclaimed her as their queen, Rose felt confident again that she could win Bitter Creek back.

She met him on the stairway as she was going down to breakfast. He came no longer to her room, but she knew he was going regularly to Amaryllis' room.

"Good morning," she greeted him cheerfully.

"Good morning, Rose," he answered and she detected a note in his voice she had not heard for some time.

Amaryllis now appeared at her doorway, calling, "Wait for me, Bitter Creek."

Rose looked up at her. Amaryllis was, as usual, flawlessly lovely—blonde and fresh, her hair a crisp pale gold, her smooth skin petal-fresh and her eyes, blue.

And yet, looking at her now, Rose saw something about the woman that did not add up to beauty.

At the moment of Rose's discovery, Bitter Creek did a strange thing. He walked on ahead of Amaryllis, ignoring her call for him to wait.

Rose's heart soared with hope. The spell Amaryllis had cast over Bitter Creek was dissolving.

Rose later asked him what kind of warning Cattle Annie and Little Britches had given the gang.

"Rose, you were right about not trusting that damned Bloody Turner. Cattle Annie saw him with a bunch of lawmen," he said.

"I just felt that there was something not right about that redhead," Rose answered and felt happier than she had for many weeks.

"I expect there'll be a raid on Ingalls one of these days," Bitter Creek went on. "Those deputies will be riding in here expecting to clean out the whole Doolin gang."

"But you're ready for them, aren't you?" she asked.

He smiled down at her. "Ready and waiting," he shot back. "Ready and waiting."

"Did you know Daniel has been courting Amanda?" she asked now.

He was immediately interested. "You mean the waitress?"

"She's a sweet girl and Daniel loves her."

"And Bree? Have you heard anything about Bree and your pa and that wanton Mary Kahns?" he asked.

"Oh, Bitter Creek, I've missed being able to talk to you about my family," she whispered.

"I know, and I missed hearing about them," he answered. "Tell me, what's the latest about the love triangle?"

"You make it sound so romantic." She laughed. "I haven't heard anything. I'd like to take a ride out there sometime. Would you go with me?"

"I'd like that," he agreed. "How about tomorrow?"

She made her plans carefully. She intended, after paying a visit to Pa, to persuade Bitter Creek to go with her to the secret woodland room where they had first loved.

She would remind him that it was there he had taken her maiden's veil. She would remind him how he had once loved her.

They left early the next day. A perfect late-summer morning was just beginning. The east was flushed with beautiful pink light against which crimson bars shone across the sky, and the dew was thick on the grass in front of the hotel.

Rose sat close beside Bitter Creek on the buggy seat as they drove through the exquisite morning.

Quail were drimming and birds chirping.

"I'm glad we're going out to Pa's together," Rose said, smiling at him.

"Me, too," he answered.

"I love you," she decided to say suddenly.

He looked at her for a long moment before he spoke. "It used to make me angry for you to say that, but now I like it."

"Oh, Bitter Creek, I do love you with all my heart. I was heartsick when you were with Amaryllis."

He did not answer and they rode in silence for a while.

Presently she spoke. "Did you love her?"

"I was flattered by her attention," he answered frankly.

"She is beautiful," Rose faltered.

"No, she isn't," he declared definitely. "No, Rose, she isn't beautiful. Beauty has to shine from within, and inside, Amaryllis Meadows is hard and scheming."

"You slept with her?" blurted Rose.

"Yes, I slept with her. I know I promised to always be true to you, but, Rose, a man can forget a promise when he is in heat."

"In heat?"

"Yes, a man can forget any promises he might have made. He sees a woman who flatters him and tells him she cannot live unless she goes to bed with him and he gives in. It is as simple as that."

"I've been true to you," she flared.

"I know, honey. I know. All I can say is that I'm sorry."

"Sorry!" she echoed. "I loved you. I trusted you."

When he spoke again it was to say mildly, "Rose, will you be my sweetheart again?"

And she said simply, "Yes, I love you."

The old farmhouse looked more dilapidated than ever as they rode up.

"Looks deserted," commented Bitter Creek as he helped Rose from the buggy.

They went up to the door and knocked.

There was no answer.

Then suddenly Ira appeared at the side of the house. He was slobbering and his mouth was open to display two rows of rotten teeth.

"Ma's out in the barn," he reported.

"Is he half-witted or not?" Bitter Creek

whispered to Rose.

"I don't know," she whispered back. "Sometimes he makes pretty good sense and then again, he slobbers so."

They followed the boy to the ramshackle barn and entered quietly, looking around for Mary Kahns.

They heard a snicker and laughter and looked around to see where the sound came from.

Rose saw Mary Kahns's red hair first. She was naked and rolling around in the hay.

By her side, with a short jacket on, was Bree.

Rose and Bitter Creek and Ira stood watching. The two, engaged in touching each other and kissing, were unaware of their audience.

Ira broke the silence. "Ma," he screeched. "Ma."

She sat upright, her great breasts bouncing like balls as she snarled, "What the hell do you want?"

Rose gave Bree one long withering stare, turned on her heel, and left, followed by Bitter Creek. Ira stayed to watch.

Back in the buggy, Bitter Creek asked if she would like to visit Rebecca, Bill, Ellie, and the boys.

"Not now," she answered sadly. "Not after what we've just seen. I want to go to our secret woodland dell. I just want to stay in its quietness awhile with you."

The dell was just as she remembered it. It was scented with flower fragrance and the sun, filtering through the giant trees, cast lacy shadows below.

Rose stood for a long moment silently, then she clasped Bitter Creek's hand.

"Remember how it was, darling?" she asked. "Remember that first time? I was a virgin and you took my maiden's veil."

"I remember," he said softly. "I remember it all."

"Bitter Creek, I know you can't understand why I've been afraid to be married, but I do love you. Will you repeat our vows here?"

He was puzzled. "Vows?" he questioned. "What kind of vows?"

"Just you and me before God. I remember the words from when Edith and Bill got married. I memorized the words," she said softly, reverently.

"If you wish, honey," he answered.

"Repeat after me," she said solemnly. "I, Bitter Creek Newcomb, take thee, Rose Dunn, for my lawfully wedded wife."

"I, Bitter Creek Newcomb, take thee, Rose Dunn, for my lawfully wedded wife," he repeated slowly.

She continued, "To have and to hold from this day forward, for better, for worse."

He repeated the words.

"For richer, for poorer, in sickness and in health, to love and to cherish," she intoned.

"For richer, for poorer, in sickness and in health, to love and to cherish," he said.

She went to him then and whispered, "Till death us do part."

"Till death us do part," he said softly. "And now, it's your turn."

"I, Rose Dunn, take thee, Bitter Creek Newcomb, for my lawfully wedded husband, to have and to hold from this day forward, for better, for worse, for richer, for poorer, in sickness and in health, to love and to cherish, till death us do part."

She stretched out on the soft mossy grass then and invited him to love her.

She gave herself completely to him, her body and her heart, and when it was over, he lay panting.

"Is it because we went through a ceremony that you gave every part of yourself to me?" he asked curiously.

"I don't know, darling," she whispered. "I know only that I love you. And I want to please you. When you nibble at my breasts, I want only to have you drive deep within me, to make us truly, truly one."

On the way back to town, he said simply, "Honey, you know the ceremony we went through isn't a legal ceremony?"

"I know, but I feel that now we are truly one; and someday I'll want the other kind of ceremony. Just seeing Bree today, though, brings it all back—the way I always felt about marriage and the way Pa used to bore into Ma."

Chapter 23

Amaryllis was waiting for them when they got back to the hotel.

She was rigid with anger as she demanded, "Where the hell have you been?"

Bitter Creek motioned for Rose to go on into the hotel.

She went inside but stood by the door so she could hear.

Amaryllis repeated her question, "Where the hell have you been?"

His voice was hard and mean as he rasped, "Since when do I have to account to you for my time?"

"Since you made love to me," she shrilled.

He turned away and she made a lunge for him, grabbing him by the shoulders.

"Don't you turn your back on me," she cried. "You made me think you loved me. You made me think you cared for me and now you throw me aside for that . . . that—"

"Shut up," Bitter Creek muttered.

"I went up to the holy house," she ranted on.

"You what?" Bitter Creek asked, shocked.

"I walked right up to that precious front door

and who should come to the door but the great one himself, Bill Doolin," she rambled on.

Bitter Creek stared at the woman aghast.

"Thought maybe I'd get a glimpse of the holy lady, the one and only angelic Edith."

"You're drunk," Bitter Creek declared as Amaryllis released her hold on him and staggered.

"Had to be drunk to get up my nerve to go up to the holy house to look for my lover," she declared loudly.

"You make me sick," he retorted and walked away in the direction of the Doolins'.

Amaryllis looked around at the people who had gathered to listen to her tirade and she laughed. "Quite a show wasn't it? Well, you ain't seen nothin' yet. I'll really give that Bitter Creek hell tonight."

Rose later warned Bitter Creek of Amaryllis' threat.

This was to be the last big dance before the gang departed on the bank robbery Bill Doolin had been planning.

Cattle Annie and Little Britches were present and Bill Doolin was fiddling away.

Edith Doolin, as usual, was not present. Rose wondered what the woman did alone in that little white house.

The dance was in full swing and Rose was being passed around from partner to partner when Amaryllis made her appearance.

She was dressed in pale blue and there was a sprig of artificial blue flowers tucked in her golden hair.

Kate was evidently watching for her because she hurried across the dance floor to meet her. "Honey, I don't think you're feelin' too good this evening. Why don't you go upstairs?"

"Now, Mamma," Amaryllis gushed, "don't you be tellin' your daughter what she should do. It's kind of late for that, don't you think?"

Rose was surprised to note that Amaryllis had called Kate, "Mamma." Before it had always been a long drawn out plaintive cry of "Mother."

"You've had too much to drink," Kate hissed. "You get back upstairs."

"Ha, ha, ha, ha," Amaryllis squealed. "Mamma says I've had too much to drink."

Red Buck wobbled over to where Amaryllis stood and took her arm, "Come on, sweetheart, let's you and me go out into the other room."

She shook his arm off. "You drunken pig," she vented angrily. "Leave me alone."

By this time, the music had been stilled and everyone was listening.

Kate stood nearby, plainly embarrassed, her lovely face flushed.

Amaryllis struck a pose and grinned at her audience.

"Please go to your room," Kate begged.

"Shut up, Mamma," Amaryllis responded.

"Amaryllis, please," her mother begged. "This is to be the last big dance for a while. Don't spoil it. Everyone wants to have a nice time."

"Nice time, hell!" Amaryllis flared. "I came to Ingalls to see my mamma. My beautiful mamma who was supposed to be the Queen of the Barbary Coast."

"Amaryllis," Kate groaned and turned white as a ghost.

"Hell, Mamma, you ain't never been the Queen of the Barbary Coast. You ain't never been the queen of nothin' unless it was the queen of some slum joint like The Brass Lantern."

"Hush," her mother implored.

"You told all these folks you was the Queen of the Barbary Coast. You lied, Mamma, you lied."

Bill Doolin ran his bow across his violin as a signal for the group to dance, but Amaryllis raced across the floor and jerked the instrument from his fingers.

"No, you don't, Bill Doolin," she screamed. "You might be king to all these men, but you ain't no king to me. You ordered me out of your house today. Yes, you did, and you didn't have no call to do that. You're just hidin' that woman of yours from the world."

She looked around at the crowd and snorted. "Yeah, you're hidin' her from the world just like my mamma hid me from the world. She thought she was keepin' me safe in that second-rate boarding school. Hah! I was goin' to bed with the handyman when I was fourteen."

Kate's face had now turned ashen and she fled from the huge room.

"That's right, Mamma, run away," Amaryllis called. "Run away. That's what you did. You ran away from Spider McCall. You ran away and left that man flat. Of course, he wasn't much to run away from, but I think that Spider McCall was my pa."

"You're crazy," Red Buck spoke up now. "And you're a no-good daughter to talk like that to your mamma."

Bill Doolin snatched his violin away from Amaryllis, who stood swaying unsteadily before him, and began to play a lively tune. The dancing began again.

Amaryllis stood sniveling before Bill Doolin for a while; then she staggered out of the room.

Chapter 24

The hotel was very quiet the next morning. The men who stayed there, members of the Doolin gang, were resting, preparatory to leaving early the following morning.

Rose, snuggled in Bitter Creek's arms, relished every moment of this time together.

"How long do you think you'll be gone?" she asked, kissing him.

He reached down to clasp one of her bare breasts and then bent down to kiss it tenderly.

"I love you," she whispered.

He kissed the other breast and then straightened to draw her close. She felt the hardness of him and squirmed.

"Not again?" he questioned.

"Yes, again and again and again," she begged. "We're going to be apart and I can't stand to be without your love. It's been hell these past weeks when you were with Amaryllis."

"Hush, my darling," he whispered. "We are going to forget all about that. We are going to forget that we were ever apart. We are together again and that's all that counts."

By evening, after the Doolin gang had departed, the town seemed strangely deserted.

Amaryllis was sulking in her room as Kate and Rose manned the registration desk.

"Poor Amaryllis." Kate sighed. "She must hate herself this morning."

Rose doubted that, but said nothing.

Kate seemed lost in thought, then asked, "Did you hear her mention Spider McCall?"

Rose nodded.

"She's right. Spider McCall is her pa. Spider McCall," she went on sadly. "Just the mention of his name brings it all back. Such a long time ago and I was so young."

"You met him in California?"

"Yes. As I told you I left the gold fields with my lover, Stony Brown. Well, we parted company after a few months and I met up with Spider," she reminisced.

"You loved this Spider?" Rose asked.

"I worshiped him," Kate said dreamily. "He was everything I ever wanted. He was a short man, with eyes as black as the rich Kansas earth. He had broad shoulders and black curly hair and I loved him."

"What happened?"

"Well, I got in the family way and Spider had no desire to be a pa. He walked out on me. I had my little Amaryllis and I loved her. It was tough trying to raise her. I was workin' the saloons so I had an Indian woman taking care of her."

Rose listened in silence.

"That was all right when she was little, but

when she got older I put her in this school. It was the best I could afford."

"Did you ever hear from Spider McCall again?" Rose asked.

"No. He faded out of my life, but I loved that man. There's never been anyone else for me."

"How did Amaryllis suspect that he was her pa?" Rose queried.

"Gossip, I guess. She hung around The Brass Lantern now and then as she was growing up. I couldn't keep her at that school on holidays and during the summer, you know."

"What do you suppose Amaryllis will do now?"

Kate shrugged her shoulders wearily. "I don't know. I wish she'd show some gumption and give us a hand out here. With Amanda leaving, we could use the help."

"I don't suppose Amaryllis wants to be a waitress," Rose commented dryly.

"No, she's got her head in the clouds. She thought she could get your man, Bitter Creek, and that would solve all her problems."

"I know," Rose whispered.

"Problems aren't solved that easily," Kate went on. "We usually make our own problems."

"I'll be glad when the gang gets back," Rose said presently as the two worked on the ledgers.

"Have you noticed how quiet it is?" Kate asked.

"Yes. There's an air of something about to happen." Rose sighed.

"I feel it, too."

"You don't suppose those deputies or lawmen will swoop down on us—the ones Cattle Annie and

Little Britches are always reporting they see?" Rose asked.

"No," Kate answered definitely. "They don't want us. They want the gang."

"Those lawmen will never get the gang," Rose said lightly. But her voice was trembling.

"No, Bill Doolin is too smart to ever get caught," Kate observed firmly.

"I wonder . . . I wonder how his wife feels about waiting up there alone in that little white house," Rose pondered.

"It must be lonely for her. What does she do all day? One can only do so much dusting and sweeping and cooking."

"It took some guts for Amaryllis to go there," Rose said.

"She was drunk or she wouldn't have had the nerve," Kate answered.

When an itinerant preacher, Rev. Enos Perry, chanced by the following week, Amanda and Daniel decided to be married by him there in the hotel. It was a simple ceremony. Kate Meadows and Rose served as witnesses and afterward Kate served cake and coffee to the wedding party.

Suddenly, while the wedding guests were enjoying their refreshments, Amaryllis appeared in the doorway of the dining room to ask, "Can your bastard daughter come to the party, Mamma?"

That evening, Amaryllis came into the dining room again, this time wearing Amanda's waitress apron. She smiled cockily at Kate and Rose and said, "How do you like your new waitress, Mamma?"

She was a beautiful but sullen waitress. She snarled at the customers and was rude when taking their orders. Nonetheless business went along pretty much as usual until one beautiful late-fall day when the trees were brilliant in crimson and gold colors, and Timber Matt Hurd signed the register.

Rose was at the registration desk when he signed the book, looked at her with appreciation and said, "Hello, beautiful."

She smiled at him and assigned him a room as Kate came down the stairs.

Kate paused and stared at the newcomer.

He had picked up a small carpetbag and turned toward the stairs.

Kate looked down at him and her face was frozen with amazement. She stood waiting as she approached.

He tipped his hat, smiled, and said, "This place is a place of beautiful women."

He went on up the stairs and Kate came down slowly, woodenly.

"Who is that?" she asked Rose who was closing the registration book.

"He signed as Timber Matt Hurd," Rose said opening the book to show Kate.

"He is the image of Spider McCall," she said as she went to a chair and sat down. Her eyes were dazed, fixed on far space.

"He's very handsome," Rose put in softly.

"Yes. Yes," she said nervously. "He has the same

145

dark curly hair, the same black eyes, the dark skin, the square body. He is the image of Spider."

Rose's first thought was of Amaryllis. "Does Amaryllis remember Spider McCall?"

"She may have a vague recollection," Kate said with uncertainty. "It's been such a long, long time ago."

"Maybe he'll be gone before she sees him," Rose said hopefully.

"Did he say how long he is staying?"

"No, he said nothing, just signed the register and smiled."

"Looking at him, it was just as though the years had turned back. I was young again and it was Spider, with his black eyes, looking at me."

"Do you suppose he could be a lawman?" Rose presently asked.

Kate shrugged.

Mr. Hurd was in the dining room that evening. His suit was well pressed and he was all smiles as he greeted Rose and Kate.

Then Amaryllis came into the room. The tight apron she wore revealed every curve of her enticing body. She went straight to his table and stood, smiling down at him.

"I can't believe my eyes," he said softly. "Three of the most beautiful women on earth in one room!"

Amaryllis laughed, but her eyes were feverish with excitement as she said, "You remind me of someone I knew many years ago."

"It couldn't have been *many* years ago," the

man said gallantly. "You are very young."

"He was dark as you are dark and his eyes were black and he had square shoulders," Amaryllis said in a low tone.

"And you were in love with him?" the man asked.

"No, I hated him because he loved my mamma," she said bitterly.

He gave his order then for a thick steak and Rose thought she had never heard such a well-modulated voice.

As he ate, he glanced at Amaryllis, who was waiting on other customers. When she came to his table, he asked, "You do not like your job?"

"I hate it," she cried.

"Then why stay here?" he questioned. "You have beauty and youth. You could go anywhere."

"I have been everywhere and I have seen everything," she rasped and left to go to another table.

As he was leaving the dining room, he remarked to Rose, "Your friend is not a happy person."

Rose did not answer. There seemed nothing to say.

Kate approached them then and asked, "Mr. Hurd, how long are you going to be with us?"

"Just a little while," he answered, smiling and showing his teeth white as curd.

"What business are you in, sir?" Kate asked.

"I am a cattle buver, ma'am," he said and smiled again in a friendly fashion as he headed for the door.

Amaryllis stood, staring after him.

Chapter 25

The two became inseparable. Amaryllis followed Timber Matt wherever he went.

She seemed like one hypnotized by his charm.

"You don't suppose Amaryllis will tell Timber Matt about the gang being gone on a job?" Rose asked Kate one day.

"Honey, I suspect Amaryllis has told him anything and everything he wants to know."

"But what if he is a lawman?" Rose asked.

"We'll have to keep our eyes open and see what happens," Kate said matter-of-factly. "Perhaps he is what he says he is, a cattle buyer."

"You know you don't believe that," Rose countered.

"I know," Kate answered sadly. "I think I'll have a talk with Amaryllis."

Rose sighed. She knew Amaryllis would only snarl at Kate if she tried to talk with her about the danger of telling Timber Matt the secrets of Ingalls.

No doubt, Amaryllis had revealed that Ingalls was the headquarters for the Doolin gang and that the little white house at the end of town was the home of Bill Doolin and his bride, Edith.

"I was thinking," Rose said and stopped. "If Timber Matt is a lawman he could swoop down on the Doolin house and take Edith—"

"I thought of that, too," Kate interrupted. "Bill Doolin would be a raging bull if anyone touched his precious Edith."

"You had better talk to Amaryllis and tell her what will happen if anyone gets near Bill Doolin's wife."

"I will," Kate promised.

Kate reported back later to Rose.

"I went to Amaryllis' room. I was surprised to find her there," Kate said wiping her eyes. "She was lying on her bed, like a big crumpled doll."

Rose, listening, said nothing.

"My poor, beautiful Amaryllis." Kate sighed before continuing.

"She's always with Timber Matt in the late afternoons," Rose said slowly. "What happened that she wasn't with him today?"

"I don't know; only she seemed sad somehow and broken."

"You don't suppose he's left town?" Rose put in uncertainly. "He hasn't checked out of the hotel?"

"No, I saw him at the bar when I went upstairs," Kate said.

"Anyway, Amaryllis looked up at me. She had been crying and she said, 'Mamma, I'm sorry for everything.' And she put out her hand and touched my hand."

Rose was amazed. "She's been so mean and angry and seemed to hate everyone except Timber Matt."

"You know, Rose, I've been thinking about his name. I know cowboys and ranch hands and outlaws take these crazy nicknames, but Timber Matt doesn't fit this man."

"I thought that from the very first day he signed the register," Rose exclaimed.

"So I said, 'Amaryllis, honey, I'm sure you haven't told your friend, Timber Matt, about the Doolin gang using Ingalls as their hideout.'"

"What did she say?" Rose asked eagerly.

"She didn't answer me straight out," Kate conceded wearily.

"And then I begged her never to tell Timber Matt about the Doolin house. I told her Bill Doolin would kill anyone who went there. She smiled when I said that and admitted he was almost mad enough to kill her when she went there that day looking for Bitter Creek."

"I wonder if she's told him everything," Rose mused now.

"She wouldn't say. So the only thing we can do is warn Bitter Creek when the gang returns."

"Do you suppose Amaryllis loves this Timber Matt?" Rose asked.

"I'm sure she does. I think she is mad about him," Kate said. "I think, like mother like daughter. Just as I was so attracted to Spider Mc-Call so many years ago, so my Amaryllis is attracted to a man who looks enough like him to be his twin."

"Do you think she will go with him when he leaves?"

"Sure, if he asks her, but he won't. His kind love

150

and then leave them."

"Are they lovers, do you think?" Rose asked suddenly.

"Amaryllis has the same hot blood in her veins that I have," Kate conceded slowly. "Of course, she's taken him to her bed. Why not? She is so in love and I know it will break her heart when he leaves her."

"I can't understand what changed her so."

"Perhaps because she's so in love. When I left her, I begged her again not to tell Timber Matt anything about the Doolin gang but she just smiled kind of mysteriouslike and said, 'Mamma, trust me.' "

"If only Bitter Creek would come back," Rose whispered.

Kate said nothing at the moment, but later, when she passed close to Rose in the dining room, she said very low, "There's something about to happen. I can feel it in the air."

Chapter 26

The fall morning dawned dark with clouds and threatening rain. Hollyhocks and late roses were in bloom and dripped shining beads of dew. An occasional wild gust of wind brought down masses of oak leaves.

Amaryllis and Timber Matt having just returned from a buggy ride, Amaryllis now entered the lobby of the hotel. She smiled sweetly at Kate.

"Did you have a nice ride?" Kate asked. "You were lucky it hasn't started to rain."

"Yes, we had a lovely ride, Mamma," Amaryllis said.

Timber Matt bowed to Amaryllis and Kate, then went off in the direction of the bar.

"Isn't he handsome, Mamma?" Amaryllis asked.

"Yes, he is very handsome," Kate agreed.

"Was my pa like him? Did he look like him and did he have his charming ways?"

"Yes, he was very much like Matt. You don't mind if I drop the 'Timber' part? He doesn't seem like a Timber Matt to me," Kate explained.

"It's all right, Mamma. You can call him Matt if you like."

"Are you in love with him?" Kate asked in a low tone.

"I love him, Mamma. I love him just as you must have loved Spider McCall. And now I can understand how much you must have loved him."

"Amaryllis, don't let Matt get you in the family way. He'll desert you just as Spider deserted me when I needed him."

Amaryllis was instantly belligerent. "Just because they look alike is not reason they are alike."

"I'm just warning you, honey," Kate said.

"Well, don't warn me," Amaryllis answered darkly. "I'm a big girl and I can take care of myself."

Amaryllis and Matt were in the dining room later; their heads were close together and they were whispering.

Rose, as she served Grandpa Ellis who had come in for a bowl of stew, heard Matt say, "It won't be such an exciting life for you, my darling."

And she saw Amaryllis' bright color flush up. Her eyes were stars.

"I wonder if he's asking her to go away with him," she confided to Kate later.

"Poor Amaryllis. Men like Matt Hurd never give. They only take," Kate mourned.

"Maybe he truly loves Amaryllis. She must believe everything he says."

"He could tell her Ingalls is located on the coast of California and she would believe him." Kate sighed.

"I wonder how it will all end," Rose mused.

"Well, there're only two ways it *can* end," Kate said practically. "He will leave alone and leave her broken-hearted or he will take her with him if and when he leaves. I would hate to see her heart broken," she said very low, with a trembling voice. "I remember how I cried and cried when Spider left me."

The days went by and the gang did not return.

Rose was worried but she stifled her impulses to visit the little white house to talk to Edith, to perhaps find comfort in their loneliness together.

She waited.

And then one late-fall day when the first hint of winter was in the air, Bill Eckridge came to the hotel. He was wild-eyed and evidently at a loss for words.

"Is Rebecca all right?" Rose questioned quickly. "Or is it Ellie or Hank or Link?"

"It's Pa," Bill stated.

"Pa?" Rose echoed. "Is he sick?"

"No, he came to our place the other night. Bree kicked him out," Bill said.

"Kicked him out!" Rose cried stunned. "How could he kick Pa off his own farm?"

"Bree just ran him off," Bill continued definitely. "Bree told Pa to 'git' and Pa came to our place, mad as a hornet."

"I suppose so," Rose said slowly. "Is Pa at your place now?"

"Yes, and he wouldn't give me no peace until I came into Ingalls and got the marshal," Bill went on. "Pa raves and rants and takes on somethin' awful."

"And what about Mary Kahns? What did she do?" Rose asked.

"I guess she didn't do nothin'. I don't guess she really cares," he said in disgust.

"I'll bet she cares," Rose declared hotly. "I'll bet she's the one that put Bree up to kicking Pa out. She was probably tired of Pa and his mean ways and Bree is younger and strong."

Kate, who had been listening quietly to this recital, now said, "It seems to me you've got to get that old man's farm back for him." She looked shrewdly at Bill, then asked, "You ain't too anxious for the old man to live with you, are you?"

Bill rolled his eyes upward. "No, ma'am," he said emphatically.

"Well, we need a man to be the marshal," Kate said. "I've got plenty of tin stars here in this drawer. They've come in handy."

"Bree knows all the old men in town and he knows they aren't marshals," Rose pointed out.

"There's one he doesn't know," Kate said. "There's only one man in town who can act the part."

Rose looked puzzled. But when Kate continued, she grinned.

"That's Matt Hurd," Kate stated. "Bree ain't never seen Matt. Matt can go out there and put that old man back on his farm."

"If he'll do it," Rose said.

"Well, we've already talked about how he looks like a lawman," Kate said briskly. Her eyes flashed a message to Rose. "Let's see how he looks with a tin star pinned on him."

Bill, anxious to get back, paced the floor while they waited for Amaryllis and Matt to return from their walk.

When the couple came back, Kate explained the situation out at the Dunn farm.

When she had finished, Amaryllis declared flatly, "Matt doesn't want any part of such carrying on. Just leave him out of it."

"Do you mean that this woman, Mary Kahns, has probably persuaded your brother-in-law, Bree, to kick your pa out?" Matt asked Bill when Kate had finished the telling.

"Yes," said Bill vigorously. He was nervous and anxious to get back.

"What sort of woman is this Mary Kahns?" Matt asked curiously.

Rose put in now, "She's a great big heifer of a woman. She's got red hair and Pa brought her home after Ma died and she moved right into his bed."

Matt laughed. "Sounds like she's a go-getter. And she's got a home no matter which one wins out."

"And she's got a son who's a half-wit and slobbers," Rose added.

"Sometimes I wonder if he's as daft as he pretends to be," Bill contended now. "He came over to the farm off and on during the summer and he was always trying to get Link or Hank to go out in the barn with him."

"Not so dumb, eh?" Matt grinned.

"He's mean besides."

Amaryllis spoke now. "I don't want Matt to go

out there. It's none of our business. From what I've heard he's a mean old man. I heard you had to crawl out the window to get away from him."

"No, I didn't have to crawl out the window," Rose said sharply. "That was just some gossip around town. I don't know who started that story."

"Well, anyway, I don't want Matt getting mixed up in it," Amaryllis said, going to him and standing in front of him with her fingers resting lightly against his coat collar.

Matt turned toward Kate now. "Where's that tin star, Mrs. Meadows? Let's see how I would look as a lawman." He laughed.

"This is serious," Amaryllis shrilled. "You could get killed out there."

He put a quick light kiss on the crown of her blond hair and went to the registration desk where Kate waited with a star in her hand.

She pinned it on him and said lightly, "I deputize you as a lawman for the town of Ingalls, Oklahoma."

"That sounds official enough," he joked. "Make way for Lawman Matt Hurd!"

"Do you want me to go along?" Rose asked.

"No, this is a man's job," Matt said as he and Bill Eckridge left the lobby of the hotel.

Chapter 27

After Hurd and Eckridge left, Amaryllis was angry. She rushed upstairs to fling herself across the bed.

"I like him," Kate declared. "I thought maybe he would act embarrassed when I suggested he put the tin star on, but he didn't bat an eyelash."

"I like him, too," Rose admitted. "I hope he isn't a real lawman."

"Me, too."

Presently, Amaryllis came downstairs and just sat there glaring at Rose and her mother.

"If my Matt gets hurt it's your fault," she told Rose.

"You ought to be proud of him," Kate pointed out. "He went out there to help an old man out."

"It ain't none of his business and he ought to stay out of it." Amaryllis pouted. She went again and again to the door to peer out to see if Matt was coming.

It was almost midnight before they heard the beat of horses' hoofs.

The women were instantly at the door. When they opened it, they felt the cool fall air, and stood shivering in the doorway waiting for Matt Hurd to appear.

First he took his horse to the stable, then, grinning he entered the lobby.

"How about a cup of hot coffee?" he asked. "It's mighty cool out there. We're going to have an early winter."

Rose hurried out to get the coffee and he called after her, "Put a big swig of whiskey in it."

She laughed and hurried to do his bidding.

Then they all went into the dining room, where Matt sat, leisurely sipping his coffee and looking at his interested audience over the rim of the cup.

"Tell us what happened," Kate demanded.

He chuckled before he began to talk. "You should have warned me about that red-headed woman."

"I did tell you something about her," Rose reminded him.

"You didn't tell me she was a red-headed demon." He laughed.

"I'm so glad you're back and that you're safe," Amaryllis put in now, going to his side and kissing him.

"I was in no danger," he said dryly. "Bill and I went directly to his place. Pa was mad and mean and ranting at everyone. Well, I let on that I was a real lawman and we were going over to the Dunn farm to move him back in."

"I guess he liked that," Rose said.

"That he did. He was delighted that the law had come to take his side. So we went on over to his farm."

He paused a moment and looked around at his audience. They were all waiting with bated breath.

"It was almost dark when we got there but Bree heard us and came out of the kitchen. He saw Pa and bellowed, 'What the hell do you want, old man? I told you to get out and that's what I meant.' "

"Bree can be mighty mean," Rose said.

"Then he saw me. He didn't pay any attention to Bill, but when he saw me he yelled, 'What the hell you doing here? Get off my place.' "

"*His* place!" Rose cried outraged.

"That's what he said, 'my place.' So I flashed my star and said, 'Show me your papers that you own this place.' He blustered around and I said 'Your pa owns this place and he's moving back in right now.' "

"And then?" Rose breathed.

"With that, the red-headed woman let out a yell and said that that old man wasn't moving back in. She didn't want to sleep with him anymore."

Rose was incredulous. "She didn't say that!"

"Yes, she did and more, but I won't embarrass you by repeating what she said. She has a filthy mouth. I finally told her to shut up. Then I took Pa by the arm and walked him into the kitchen."

"Bree just stood there and let you?" Rose questioned.

"He knew that I had the upper hand. Your Pa went to a pantry, got out a strop, and hung it by the door. When he did that Bree got mighty quiet. I told them all that I would be back and if things got out of hand again, I'd take care of it," he finished.

"How can I thank you?" Rose asked. "I can't say

I've got much love for my pa, but he *is* my pa and he shouldn't be chased out of his own house."

"I was glad to do it," Matt said sincerely. "I'll check back in a few days to see that all is well out there."

"I'll go with you if you want me to," Amaryllis offered.

He smiled, but turned the offer aside with a nonchalant shrug of his wide shoulders.

"How about another cup of coffee, Rose, with a generous slug of whiskey?" he asked.

Chapter 28

True to his word, Matt Hurd journeyed out to the Dunn farm and reported back to Rose.

"Everything is quiet," he said. "That strop, which must be symbolic of something or other, is still hanging by the door. Bree seemed subdued and the red-head had nothing to say."

"Thanks, Matt," Rose said. "I appreciate it."

And to herself, she thought, If you are a lawman, I don't care. I do like you.

As the days went by, she wondered if Matt would still be at the hotel when the gang returned. They would surely come back any day now.

She was in the sitting room, splendid with Kate's red velvet furniture and gilded mirrors, when Amaryllis and Matt entered.

At that moment, she was on her knees dusting behind a settee, and for a second, she thought about jumping up and leaving, but Amaryllis' first words stopped her.

"Matt, my dear," she stammered. "What is it?"

Rose, who was peeping out, saw the man take Amaryllis' two hands in his and hold them gathered against his breast. But he did not speak.

Amaryllis was dressed in a pale-blue silk gown

which revealed her exquisite figure. Her golden hair fell to her shoulders and her eyes were blue . . . blue . . . blue.

"How beautiful you are, my darling!" the man said. "How beautiful you are!"

"What did you want to talk to me about?" Amaryllis asked, her voice trembling.

He studied her for a moment, her hands still gathered tight in his.

"Say something, Matt," she begged, freeing herself from his clasp. As she drew away from him, her eyes darkened.

"You're not telling me you are going to leave me?" she faltered. "You can't come to tell me this now! You wouldn't dare!"

"My beautiful Amaryllis, I know I promised that you could go with me when I left Inglalls, but my dear, it wouldn't work out."

"Why wouldn't it work out?" she demanded. "I love you and you love me. Oh, I don't care about getting married. I just want to be with you," she pleaded.

The tears were streaming down her face and he took her in his arms.

Rose, watching, wished she had jumped up and revealed her presence as soon as they had entered the room. Now it was too late.

"Perhaps I'll be back someday," he promised vaguely.

Amaryllis face was very white; her breast moved stormily when she cried, "You don't care for me. You said you loved me, but you don't love me at all."

163

"I do love you," he maintained stubbornly. "I love you, but I can't take you with me."

"Then prove it. Take me with you."

He looked at her steadily for a long moment, cleared his throat as if he would speak, then was silent again.

"My life is a rough one. I have no home," he said presently.

"That doesn't matter," she said shortly.

"You would get tired of living the way I must live," he went on.

"I wouldn't. I would be happy just being with you," she burst out impatiently.

Then, seeing the set expression on his face, she was quiet.

When she spoke again, it was to reproach him in a low trembling voice. "You shouldn't have promised to take me with you."

"A man sometimes makes promises he cannot keep," he said somberly.

"And a woman gives a man her body, and she believes him when he says he loves her."

He spoke now apologetically, doubtfully. "You will be glad someday that I left without you."

"Never, never," she cried savagely.

"Never is a long time," he said briefly.

"You're afraid to take me with you," she accused.

"Perhaps I am," he said walking away. Then he came irresolutely back.

She spoke slowly, thickly, after a silence. "Coward," she blazed.

He came close to her now and said softly, "This

is good-by, Amaryllis."

She raised shadowed eyes to his and spoke in a lifeless tone. "Good-by, Matt."

He stepped closer now and took her in his arms for a very brief moment, holding her close.

"Good-by, my darling," he whispered.

Then he was gone and Amaryllis stood as one turned to stone.

Rose, in her crouched position behind the settee, thought sadly, She truly loves him.

Chapter 29

The hotel seemed strangely quiet without Timber Matt Hurd.

Amaryllis stayed in her room and when Kate took her meals to her, she saw how depressed she was. Her eyes were swollen with weeping.

Kate tried to comfort her. "He'll be back. He loves you. He thought you were the most beautiful woman he had ever seen. He'll be back."

"Do you really think so, Mamma?" Amaryllis asked. She seemed strangely broken and quiet.

Kate was definite in her prediction. "I know so."

Then the gang returned! They rode into Ingalls in the cold winter twilight shooting off their guns and giving the old Rebel yell.

Rose was at the door to greet them. Kate had whiskey ready, and Rose was instantly in Bitter Creek's willing arms.

"Back at last," he breathed holding Rose close.

"I've missed you so much," she cried.

"And I you."

"I love you so!" he said simply and she laughed joyfully, confidently.

"Now you are saying, I love you," she whispered happily.

"And I mean it," he said sincerely. "I missed you."

"The Mexican women weren't beautiful?" she teased.

"Texas," he answered very low. "And if they were beautiful, I never noticed. I thought only of you."

"Ah, my darling, you are back," she rejoiced.

Then she told him about Pa's having been ejected from the old farm and about the stranger to Ingalls, Timber Matt Hurd, who had put on a tin badge and reclaimed Pa's farm.

She finished the story by saying, "We thought, that is Kate and I thought, Matt Hurd was a lawman of some sort. But we got so we actually liked him. He reminded Kate of Spider McCall whom she knew years ago in California. Amaryllis fell in love with him and he broke her heart when he left."

He told her the trip to Texas had been a big success and Doolin was more than pleased.

Kate announced there would be a big party that night to celebrate the gang's return.

"Will Bill come?" Rose asked Bitter Creek.

"I doubt it. He's glad to be home with his Edith."

"Well, the poor thing has been sitting in that white house alone all these many weeks," Rose pointed out. "It seems to me he ought to treat her to a party."

"He may come, but I doubt it," Bitter Creek replied.

Kate told Amaryllis of the celebration that

would be held that night and urged her to come.

"Honey," she said, "you can't spend all the rest of your life mourning over a man. Come on downstairs and have a good time."

"I can't, Mamma. I miss Matt too much," Amaryllis replied. "How did you forget Spider when he left you?"

"I had to keep working. I knew you were on the way and I needed money," Kate said simply.

"Maybe I'll feel differently later." Amaryllis sighed.

"No, you will never feel any differently if you just sit around and mope," Kate advised. "You've got to live one day at a time. Now put on your best dress and come on downstairs this evening."

The party was in full swing. Bill Doolin had not appeared to play the fiddle, but old Grandpa John Kopp had been pressed into service.

Rose was enjoying herself. Dressed in her red velvet gown and wearing red velvet roses in her hair, she knew she had never looked more beautiful.

Amaryllis had come downstairs for a while. But she had added nothing to the gaiety of the evening and had presently gone back to her room.

"I wish Bill had brought Edith and come to the party," Rose told Bitter Creek when he had swooped her away from Red Buck.

"You know how he is about Edith," Bitter Creek answered.

"She must get terribly lonely in that little white house," Rose said as she had so many times before.

"I guess she isn't complaining." Bitter Creek shrugged.

The dance was suddenly interrupted by the appearance of Cattle Annie and Little Britches.

Some of the gang grabbed them and whirled them around merrily.

They were as poorly dressed as ever and each wore a nondescript gray hat pulled over her dirty locks.

Finally Cattle Annie steered Bitter Creek off the floor into a corner.

"Came fast as we could, Mr. Bitter Creek," she explained breathlessly.

"You got news?" Bitter Creek drawled.

"Sure have, Mr. Bitter Creek. I guess you're the boss seein' as how Mr. Bill Doolin ain't here," Cattle Annie said, looking around.

"No, he didn't come to the dance," Bitter Creek explained.

"We saw 'em gatherin', Mr. Bitter Creek," Cattle Annie went on, wide-eyed.

"Who?"

"We saw the lawmen. 'Twas about twenty miles east of Stillwater, which is 'bout ten miles from Ingalls," she went on gesticulating with both hands in her excitement.

"What were you doing on the other side of Stillwater?" Bitter Creek asked.

"Scoutin' for the Doolin gang," Cattle Annie answered proudly.

"Tell me exactly what you saw?"

"Saw these lawmen, about twenty of them gatherin' together. They got a covered wagon.

Little Britches and I watched 'em and then we came as quick as we could to warn the gang."

"Thanks," Bitter Creek said warmly. "I don't know what the gang would do without you two."

"Some of the men make fun of us," Cattle Annie said sadly.

"Well, when they hear of how well you served the gang tonight they won't make fun of you anymore," Bitter Creek said definitely.

"Do you want me to go to the white house where Bill Doolin lives and tell him?" Cattle Annie asked eagerly.

"No, you've done your duty. You and Little Britches stay here at the party and have a good time. In fact, all the gang deserve a good time and that's what we're going to have tonight."

"What about the lawmen comin'?" Cattle Annie asked curiously.

"They won't be in these parts tonight," Bitter Creek said definitely. "We're going to forget everything tonight, and just to have a rip-roaring good time." He grabbed Cattle Annie and began to dance with her.

Later, he told Rose the news that Cattle Annie and Little Britches had brought.

"Should you have told Bill?" she asked.

"No, I'm in charge when Bill isn't here and I wouldn't interrupt his first night home with Edith," he said firmly. "Tomorrow is another day."

Rose sighed and wondered what the morrow would bring.

Bitter Creek left their bed at the first crack of dawn. It was raining. Rose could hear the water, hitting the windows and dripping down, and the creaking of the bare tree branches in the stiff winter winds.

"Where are you going, darling?" she asked as she watched him dress hurriedly.

"To alert Bill," he answered briefly. He came to sit on the bed and put his hand warmly and strongly over hers.

"I'm so glad you're back," she said again as she had said many times since his return. "I missed . . ."

She stopped, choked by emotion. Her beautiful green eyes, ringed by shadows of anxiety, were near his own.

"My beautiful Rose," he whispered. "It will take that posse quite awhile to get here, especially pulling a covered wagon and in this rain."

"The roads will be muddy," she said hopefully.

"I'll be back as soon as Bill and I talk this over and make up a plan."

"What about the gang?"

"They need to rest. It was a long, hard drive back, all the way from Texas," he said, planting a kiss on her touseled curls and leaving.

Alone in bed, she tried to visualize Bitter Creek going up to the little house and rousing Bill Doolin and Edith.

She tried to imagine the prim Edith locked in Bill Doolin's arms, she could not. There was something untouchable about Edith. But apparently, Bill loved her.

It still irritated her that she had not been invited to the little white house. It gave her a vague sensation of hurt and heartache. She could not quite analyze it, but it was always there.

Now, in anticipation of Bitter Creek's return, she stretched her young body. She could not go back to sleep so she lay watching the rain slosh against the pane. She really did not want to sleep. It was too wonderful to lie awake, enjoying the cloudless happiness of expectation. There were magic hours to come when Bitter Creek returned from the Doolins'.

Soon he entered their room, quickly shed his clothes, and eased himself back into bed.

"What did Bill say?" she asked.

"You mean about my disturbing him and Edith?" he teased.

"Were they in bed?"

"Do you mean were they making love like we do?" He grinned.

"Were they?"

"Honey, can you imagine Edith Doolin letting herself go in bed? Can you imagine her letting Bill suck her breasts until they're raw?" he asked.

"No."

"Can you imagine Bill boring into her as I bore into you?"

"No."

He laughed. "Let's forget the Doolins and think about us. I missed the taste of your breasts. I missed the sweetness and loveliness of your body."

"Show me how much you love me," she cried

turning toward him and jutting out her bare breasts.

It was late afternoon when Bill Doolin appeared at the hotel bar. He was alone and was in a jovial mood.

"Guess Bill must have gotten some satisfaction from his missus," Arkansas Tom said.

"Better not let Bill hear you say that," Red Buck cautioned. He glanced at Bill Doolin, at the other end of the bar, talking to Bitter Creek.

"Hell, what's a woman for?" Arkansas Tom snorted.

Suddenly there was an interruption. A stranger stood at the doorway announcing that he was a deputy and had come to arrest Ragged George.

Dead silence greeted this announcement.

The men at the bar turned to look stonily at him.

"What did you say your name is?" said Bill Doolin.

"Deputy Abraham Manning," the young deputy said proudly.

"What's the charge?" Bill Doolin asked.

"Hitting an old man over the head and robbing him of his money," the deputy answered.

"How much was it?" Doolin asked.

"Forty dollars," the deputy replied.

Bill Doolin looked incredulous. "Forty dollars!" he exclaimed.

The deputy nodded.

Doolin looked at Ragged George. "Is this true, George?" he asked.

"Sure," Ragged George said proudly. "I hit him over the head to get the money to join up with you."

"Get him out of here," Bill Doolin roared. "Any man who hits an old man over the head for forty dollars can't water Bill Doolin's horses."

The gang jumped from their bar seats and fell on Ragged George. In a few minutes they had tied him up and set him on a horse.

Deputy Abraham Manning rode through the frosty cold winter afternoon triumphantly leading a horse on which sat Ragged George, cursing, his hands tied behind him.

Chapter 30

Fourteen-year-old Archie Voegele slung his skates across his shoulders and headed for the lake just outside of Ingalls. As he walked, he hoped the ice would last long enough to skate awhile. Spring could come almost overnight in Ingalls. He fancied he smelled violets in the air.

When he neared the lake, he saw a covered wagon. He edged closer to it. There were many horses tied nearby and a group of men, evidently having breakfast, were gathering around a campfire.

Although surprised to see the covered wagon and the men, laughing and talking, he proceeded onward to the lake, clamped on his skates, and took to the ice. But presently, he saw several of the men come to the edge of the lake and shout for him to come to them. Reluctantly he headed toward them.

"What you doing, boy?" one of the men demanded.

"Skating," Archie replied.

"I can see that," the man said tartly. "Do you always skate here?"

"Whenever there's ice."

"Looks like the ice will be melting soon," one of the men put in.

"Yes, sir. I can almost smell the violets coming up." Archie grinned, sniffing the air.

"Don't get smart with us," the taller of the three men said sarcastically.

"No, sir." Archie said humbly.

"Take off those skates and come with us," the man, who was evidently in command, ordered.

Archie obeyed and followed meekly behind the trio as they went toward the covered wagon.

"We're going to have to keep you here, boy," the leader of the group said.

Archie began to blubber. "I got to get home. My pa gets awful mad if I don't do my chores."

"Gets mad at you, eh?" one of those gathered around the campfire said. "My pa used to get awful mad at me if I didn't do my chores. I can still feel that hickory stick across my bare behind."

"Let the boy go," one of the others around the campfire suggested.

"He stays here until we're ready to go," the leader said definitely.

After about an hour, all of the men but two got into the wagon and Archie was released with the admonition, "Don't you tell anybody you saw us."

Archie solemnly promised and started toward Ingalls on the run.

He streaked into town, his skates clinking loudly as he ran.

"The lawmen are coming," he began to shout when he got in front of the hotel. "The lawmen are coming. They're in a covered wagon with two of 'em ridin' horses in front. The lawmen are coming."

Rose heard the commotion and came out of the hotel. On hearing Archie's warning, she ran quickly into the bar where Bitter Creek was playing poker.

She relayed Archie's words to him and Bitter Creek laid down his hand. "Too bad." He grinned. "A winning hand and I can't play it."

He spread his cards out slowly, reverently, revealing a ten, jack, queen, king, and ace of spades.

"Holy devil!" breathed Red Buck.

"A royal flush!" cried Arkansas Tom.

"Let's go, men," Bitter Creek cried. "Man your posts."

"That makes me sick," moaned Arkansas Tom. "A royal flush and you can't play it! It's bad luck, though, 'cause they're spades."

"What the hell you mean, bad luck?" asked Bitter Creek.

"Spades mean death," Arkansas Tom declared mournfully.

Bitter Creek laughed and turned to Rose. "Where's that young Paul Revere?"

"Out in front of the hotel," she answered. "Oh, darling, be careful."

He took a coin from his pocket and gave it to Rose. "Give this to that boy and tell him to run up to Bill Doolin's house and tell him the time has come."

Rose did his bidding and came back into the lobby to find the gang ready to leave.

She clung to Bitter Creek a moment; then he was gone.

She turned to find Amaryllis on the stairway.

Amaryllis' eyes were very bright as she asked, "Did I hear someone yelling that the lawmen were coming?"

"Yes," Rose answered. "The Voegele boy was down on the lake skating and he saw a covered wagon filled with lawmen. They held him prisoner for a while, but released him."

"So he spread the word," Amaryllis finished dryly.

"You aren't hoping that Matt Hurd is with the lawmen?" Rose asked incredulously.

"I can hope, can't I?" Amaryllis snapped.

"There's going to be gunfire and some of our men may be killed," Rose said slowly, but her voice was trembling.

Amaryllis' eyes were feverish with excitement. "Matt could be killed too."

Rose turned away then and went to the door to look out.

The street was empty of life, but full of ice that was beginning to melt to reveal great patches of mud.

Maybe, she thought hopefully, the covered wagon would get mired down in the mud and the lawmen would be easy pickings for the Doolin gang.

She knew Bill Doolin always had a plan for everything so she supposed he and Bitter Creek had devised some means to cope with the onslaught of the lawmen.

"Where is the gang hiding?" Amaryllis asked coming to the door.

"I wouldn't know," Rose said coldly.

"Don't get on your high horse with me," Amaryllis muttered. "If Bitter Creek was in that covered wagon, you'd be cheering him on."

"But Bitter Creek isn't in that wagon," Rose pointed out. "Bitter Creek would have better sense than to be in that wagon."

Kate came down the stairs now. "Arkansas Tom is sick upstairs," she reported. "I wonder if he's really sick or if he's a coward."

"He's no coward," Rose said definitely. "None of Bill Doolin's men are cowards. Maybe he really is sick. He looked sick when Bitter Creek's royal flush was spades."

"I know he's very superstitious," Kate conceded. "I remember a bird hit a window here one time and Arkansas Tom wouldn't leave the hotel all day. Swore it was a sign of death."

Kate went to join Rose and Amaryllis at the front door.

"Street's deserted," she said. "Everything is so quiet."

"Too quiet," Amaryllis breathed.

Then they saw the town doctor's son, Richard Dragg, come out of his house and go to the town pump.

"Fill your bucket and get back home," Kate commanded.

"He can't hear you," Amaryllis said.

"I know. I know," Kate answered. "But I want him to hurry. He could be killed out there in the middle of the street."

The boy filled his bucket and began to lug it

back to his home.

Kate called to him, "Richard, get off the street."

He sat the bucket down and called back, "What did you say, Mrs. Meadows?"

Kate yelled again, louder this time, "Get off the street."

The boy looked puzzled, but picked up the filled bucket and went on to his house.

The three women waited now, eyes riveted on the far end of Main Street.

Chapter 31

After what seemed an interminable wait, they heard the sound of a creaking wagon.

"It's the covered wagon," Rose breathed and felt her heart lurch with fear.

The covered wagon came into view now, slowly, as the mud was deep in places.

"They are sitting pigeons," Kate said flatly.

The two horsemen on either side of the wagon sat erect and seemed to be fearless.

As they came directly in line with the hotel, Kate gasped, "Matt Hurd!"

Amaryllis recognized the horseman at the same time. She bolted out the door into the street.

"Matt, Matt," she screamed. "It's an ambush. Matt, it's an ambush."

Matt's face froze when he saw her, but he said nothing.

There was the sharp sound of gunfire from the wagon and an answering volley came from the surrounding buildings.

The battle had begun!

Amaryllis was struck and fell face down in the mud.

"Amaryllis," Kate cried and was ready to run

out the door. Rose clung to her.

"I've got to go to her," Kate screamed.

"You'll be killed if you go out there," Rose reasoned. "Wait! Oh, look, Doc Dragg is going out. He's holding up a white handkerchief and he's got Richard to help him."

"They must have seen the doctor's shingle and realized he is a doctor," Rose said as they watched the doctor and Richard half-drag and half-carry the bleeding Amaryllis into the doctor's home.

The shooting began in earnest now. Rifle barrels gleamed in the winter sun. But apparently the blacksmith was unaware of the noise outside his smithy as they could hear the measured strokes of his hammer amidst the sounds of gunfire.

The battle raged on and on.

Rose and Kate moved away from the door when they realized they were in danger of being shot. Then they noticed Arizona Tom, who had planted himself directly above them and was firing from upstairs.

All around the town revolver and rifle fire sounded. Frequently, glass was shattered; and the air was filled with the sharp sounds of gun blasts.

Rose ran upstairs to see if she could help Arizona Tom. She found him on his feet, revolver in hand, waiting. As she watched, she saw one of the lawmen run across the street. Tom fired, killing the man instantly.

Now rapid gunfire was directed at the window from which Arizona Tom had shot. Tom ducked away, but the window was splintered, and he was cut by flying glass.

"Go back downstairs, Rose," he panted. "It's a hell of a lot safer down there."

Rose went back to where Kate waited.

Kate was in a frenzy, worrying about Amaryllis.

Rose tried to comfort her but all the time she was thinking, Bitter Creek, where are you? She supposed he was on one of the nearby roofs or in the upper story of some house.

There was nothing to do but wait.

By now, Arizona Tom had killed two more lawmen so he had become the main target for those remaining.

Presently one of the lawmen, whom Rose recognized as Bloody Turner, the poker player whom Bitter Creek had liked so much, bounced into the lobby of the hotel.

"You traitor," she cried when she confronted him.

"Stand aside," he said harshly and then spoke to Kate. "Mrs. Meadows, if you do not tell that gunman upstairs to come down, we are going to burn your hotel down."

"You're bluffing," Kate sneered.

"I assure you, madam, I am not bluffing," he asserted firmly.

"He means it," Rose said.

"You wouldn't burn down a woman's livelihood?" Kate asked plaintively.

"That man upstairs has killed three lawmen," Bloody Turner shot back.

"Let me talk to him," Kate said.

"I'll give you three minutes."

Kate hurried up the stairs.

Presently she came back to report that Arizona Tom was too much of a gentleman to let the hotel be burned down. Besides, he was out of ammunition. Behind her Arizona Tom came swaggering down the stairs with upraised arms.

"That damned royal flush of Bitter Creek's started this whole mess," he was muttering. "Spades always mean bad luck."

"Don't worry, Arizona Tom," Rose comforted. "Bill Doolin will have you out of jail soon."

"Yeah, none of Bill Doolin's boys ever stay in jail for long and none's ever dangled from a rope," Arizona Tom said proudly.

Rose crept to the window to peer out. She reeled back as though struck.

"What's the matter, Rose?" Kate cried in alarm.

"It's Bitter Creek," she cried. "He's been shot. He must have tumbled off the roof of McKinley's Mercantile."

She did not mention that although he still had his six-shooter in his hand, the chambers apparently were empty.

Rose sprinted upstairs. She knew where a Winchester, holster, and bandoleer of shells were.

Kate ran after her. "Where are you going, Rose?"

"I'm going to Bitter Creek."

"You'll be killed out there," Kate screamed.

Rose ignored her words and ran to a room at the rear of the hotel. There, she took the sheets from the bed and quickly tore them into strips. She tied the strips together and anchored this makeshift ladder to a bedpost.

Quickly, she lowered the Winchester, the holster, a revolver of her own, and some shells to the ground.

Then she swung over the window sill and slid easily to the ground.

With the rifle and shells under one arm and the heavy six-shooter slapping against her thighs, she ran out into the street.

All activity stopped.

No lawman would deliberately shoot a woman. Rose was counting on that unwritten rule as she ran directly into the line of fire!

She reached the sprawling Bitter Creek safely, jerked him to an upright position, and gave him the six-shooter.

Then she knelt at his side with the Winchester.

The firing resumed.

Soon above the sound of gunfire, Doolin's voice rang out. "Hold off the posse until Rose and Bitter Creek reach the stable."

Bitter Creek was bleeding badly and was weak from loss of blood.

Rose helped him to his feet. He was so weak he staggered helplessly. Leaning him against the side of the McKinley's Mercantile, she took his gun and strapped it around her slim waist.

Then, Winchester in hand, she half-dragged and half-carried him, hugging the sides of the buildings as she went, firing the Winchester and protected by the fire of Doolin and his men.

When they reached the livery stable, Bitter Creek collapsed. Red Buck ran inside the back end of the stable and came out with Bitter Creek's horse. Rose held the animal while Red Buck helped Bitter Creek to mount.

Bitter Creek, pale and trembling, gripped the saddle horn and tried to guide the horse down a draw behind the barn.

Meanwhile, the lawmen were converging on the livery stable even though the gang was blazing away at them. Rose, waiting in the far corner, noticed that Doolin's men were making their way to the stable.

The air was so thick with gunpowder smoke that the gang held handkerchiefs over their mouths as they kept firing through the slits of the old stable.

"Our ammunition is getting low," Bill Doolin yelled. "We'll have to make a run for it."

They jumped on their horses and went out the back door.

The remaining lawmen were in hot pursuit.

A running gun battle took place.

Doolin's horse was shot in the jaw and the animal, wild with pain, reared up, but Doolin, master rider that he was, held his seat. Another shot cracked the animal's front leg. Doolin jumped clear as his prize stallion went down emitting the horrible cry of a wounded animal.

Red Buck closed in and Doolin swung up behind him. Then Doolin turned and coolly fired at the lawman who had wounded his horse, killing the man with one shot.

The gang were off and away, but at the end of the long deep draw they were stopped by a wire fence. Bitter Creek was lying by this obstacle.

Red Buck snipped the wire so they could go through while several of the gang helped Bitter Creek back on his horse. Then Doolin jumped on with Bitter Creek and held him in the saddle.

They traveled some time thus until they halted to make a crude litter of poles thrust through the sleeves of their coats. With the litter swung between their horses, they hurried as fast as possible to their hideaway, Old Rock Fort.

Rose tarried in the stable for some time.

With the gang gone, the posse had evidently decided to leave, too. When Rose went back to the hotel, she noticed that their covered wagon was gone.

In her path were dead bodies and dead horses strewn about.

Chapter 32

Shattered glass was everywhere and every building was riddled with bullets.

When Rose entered the hotel, she saw Angelica weeping.

"Everywhere there is death," the girl cried. "Look, the lovely hotel is ruined."

"Of course it isn't ruined. It will be as lovely as ever. Where's Kate?"

"At Dr. Dragg's."

"Have you heard how Amaryllis is?" Rose questioned now.

"No; the minute the lawmen left, Kate ran to the doc's," the girl answered, continuing to sniffle.

"I'll go over to Doc's and see what I can find out," Rose said. "When I come back we'll pick up some of this glass."

At Dr. Dragg's she found a scene of utter desolation.

Bodies were strewn about on the floor. Some were covered with sheets, others were moaning.

Rose saw Kate sitting near Amaryllis and she hurried to her side.

"How is she?" she whispered.

"The bullet grazed her shoulder. She'll be all

right," Kate said gratefully.

Amaryllis opened her eyes when she heard Rose's voice. "Did you see Matt?" she asked.

Rose answered truthfully. "Yes, he led the few lawmen who were left. They tried to capture the gang in the livery stable but couldn't."

Tears ran down Amaryllis' pale face. "He acted as if he didn't know me," she muttered sadly.

"He's a lawman," Kate said definitely. "A lawman is first, last, and always a lawman."

"But he said he loved me," Amaryllis mourned. "I tried to warn him that it was an ambush and he just stared at me."

Kate turned to Rose. "I'm going to stay here and help the doc. See what you can do about cleaning up the hotel."

Rose nodded and left. As she headed to the hotel, she tried not to think about Bitter Creek, but the memory of his gallantry to sit his horse flooded over her. Her poor, dear Bitter Creek wounded and smiling crookedly at her in his pain!

Back at the hotel kitchen, she instructed the cooks, the waitresses, and the laundress to help in picking up the glass.

"It's cold in here," Angelica complained.

"With all the windows out, it's bound to be cold," Rose said matter-of-factly. "Maybe I can get Grandpa Kopp to come and board them up."

"His place probably looks as bad as this," Angelica said glumly.

"His house isn't on Main Street," Rose pointed out.

Suddenly a bearded face appeared at one of the

windows. Rose jumped back, startled, then she recognized Red Buck.

He slipped in the door.

Rose grabbed him and kissed him. "I'm so glad to see you," she cried. "You bring news of Bitter Creek? How is he? Did you all get away safely?"

"Wait," he implored. "One question at a time. We got away. We found Bitter Creek at the end of the draw which got bigger and deeper the farther it went. Some damned fool had put a wire fence up at the end. We found Bitter Creek there. We made a litter and got him safely to the hideout."

"He's all right then?" she questioned eagerly.

"No; that's why I'm here. Rose, he has to have a doctor. He's lost so much blood and he's unconscious."

"I'll get Dr. Dragg," she said quickly. "But his house is filled with the wounded and dead."

"The lawmen are all gone?" he asked.

"They pulled out after the gang left the stable. They followed you," she explained.

He laughed triumphantly. "There weren't enough of those lawmen left alive to give us a good scare."

"I saw Bloody Turner stretched out next door. It looked like he was drawing his last breath," Rose said.

"Good," Red Buck rejoiced. "He had us all fooled. All but you, Rose. I remember you tried to warn us."

"Bitter Creek thought he could be trusted because he was such a good poker player," she reminisced.

"Let's you and me go over to the doc's and see if we can get him to go to Bitter Creek. He always liked to play cards with Bitter Creek."

"Everyone likes Bitter Creek," Rose said sadly.

"Maybe I'll have the pleasure of hauling Bloody Turner's body down to Dalton's Undertakers," Red Buck said hopefully.

Rose found things had quieted down next door. Most of the wounded had been cut by flying glass and, after being treated by the doctor, had departed.

Red Buck generously offered to lug the dead bodies down to Dalton's.

Rose told the doctor of Bitter Creek's wounds and his loss of blood.

He said, of course he would go. He had always liked and trusted Bitter Creek and besides, Bitter Creek was a damned good poker player. He said, "Kate can take care of things here until I get back."

At the Old Rock Fort they found Bitter Creek lying before a small fire that had been started to protect him from the chill of the night wind which penetrated the cavelike fortress.

The gang hovered around him; all were concerned.

"You've got to pull him through," Bill Doolin begged.

Rose was startled. She had never heard Bill Doolin beg for anything. His plea made her realize how close the bond was between the two men.

The doctor worked over Bitter Creek most of the night and when Bitter Creek opened his eyes it was to whisper, "Rose."

"I'm here, my darling," she said and was instantly at his side.

"My Rose," he murmured and went off to sleep.

"He'll be all right now," the doctor said. "He'll need more medicine."

"I'll bring it," Rose cried.

"I'll go with you," Red Buck said.

The doctor closed his kit and remarked, "Red, you had best go only to the outskirts of Ingalls. I heard one of those lawmen I patched up say they'd be back with more men."

"I wouldn't doubt that," Doolin said dryly. "They probably know there's a six-thousand-dollar bounty on my head. Just a year ago it was five thousand."

"Next year it will be seven thousand," one of the gang put in proudly.

"And the higher it gets, the more there are on my trail!" Bill Doolin said wryly.

Red Buck escorted the doctor and Rose to the outskirts of the town where he would wait for Rose's return.

All was quiet now in town so Rose secured the medicine and reported to Kate her intention of nursing Bitter Creek back to health.

"But isn't it cold and damp in that cave?" Kate protested. "I've heard all about that hideout at Old Rock Fort."

"It doesn't matter," Rose assured the woman. "All that matters is that Bitter Creek must get better and he will with me staying there and seeing that he eats right and takes his medicine."

In the meantime, a new posse had formed and was on the lookout for the gang. There had been rumors all over the countryside that the Doolin gang had a hideout at Old Rock Fort, but no one had ever been brave enough to go there to find out.

Now, with sufficient reinforcements and prodded on by the territory's outrage at the Battle of Ingalls, as it was called locally, the posse, determined to annihilate the Doolin gang, was on its way to search for the Old Rock Fort.

On their way they met a young girl loaded down with pistols and dressed in a man's shirt and a pair of dirty dungarees. The men in the posse supposed she was the daughter of a poor dirt farmer. One of them rode up to her and asked her where she was going.

"I'm aimin' to go home. I been visitin' a friend," she answered innocently.

"You seen any large group of men riding by?" the posse member asked.

"Ain't seen anybody," she asserted.

The man thanked her and the group rode on.

Cattle Annie pulled her horse to one side of the road and watched the posse ride by.

Then, cutting across fields and taking every shortcut she knew, she arrived at Old Rock Fort.

She alerted Bill Doolin and the gang.

Bill was not surprised at the news so Rose supposed he was prepared for this development.

"We move out immediately," he said.

"Where to?" Bitter Creek asked weakly.

"Wanted to surprise you, Bitter Creek," Bill said. "I've had the boys build us a real hideout on the Cimarron. It's well hidden. It's got bunks in it and will be warm in the wintertime. Not like this drafty hole."

Rose had supposed the rest of the gang was at their other hideout, Creek Nation Cave but those who were still at Old Fort Rock, insisted on again making a litter for Bitter Creek. Then they set out to make their way to the new hideaway on the Cimarron.

Chapter 33

Just as Bill Doolin had said, the new hideout was snug and warm. It had bunks built into the sides of the walls and there was a stove installed for cooking.

Two days later, Rose told Bill Doolin she must go into Ingalls for medicine and she would get food while she was there as their supply was running low.

"Be careful," he cautioned. "They'll be on the lookout for you. They may try to follow your trail."

"I'll be careful," she promised.

"I know you will, Cimarron Rose," he said.

"Cimarron Rose," she echoed. "I like that."

"The gang decided to call you that." Bill Doolin went on smiling. "They thought you should have a nickname to go along with Bitter Creek's."

"My Cimarron Rose." Bitter Creek spoke up now from his bunk bed.

On impulse, Rose turned back as she started to leave. "Bill, would you like me to deliver a message to Edith for you?" she asked.

He frowned and Rose started to leave; then went back to Bitter Creek and kissed him hard on the lips. "I love you," she whispered.

"Wait a moment," Bill Doolin said. "I will send a message. Edith must be terribly worried."

He scribbled on a piece of paper, folded it up carefully, and handed it to Rose.

As she rode toward Ingalls, she thought what a strange man Bill Doolin was. He professed to love his wife, Edith, dearly and yet he would let her stay in Ingalls alone, no doubt worrying about him. She had not seen Edith since the day Edith and Bill Doolin were married. She wondered if Edith would be glad to see her.

When she reached Ingalls, she visited Kate, who was delighted that she had come.

Amaryllis stared at her sullenly and said, "I guess you're angry yet because I tried to warn Matt that it was an ambush."

"No, Amaryllis, I'm not angry. I'm just glad your plan failed."

"I'm not," Amaryllis rasped.

"For shame," Kate spoke up.

"I would do it again," Amaryllis cried.

"He acted as though he had never laid eyes on you before," Kate reminded her daughter.

Amaryllis turned away then angrily.

Rose picked up the medicine and the food, and proceeded to the little white house. She looked around often to see that she was not observed. But apparently the posse was searching the highways and byways for the gang and knew that they had left Ingalls.

As Rose went up the walk to the door of the little white house, she felt that she was on hallowed ground. She remembered how many times she had criticized Bill Doolin for keeping his wife sequestered and isolated from people including herself as well as the gang.

She knocked on the door and waited.

Presently she heard footsteps and when the door was slowly opened, she saw Edith staring at her.

Rose spoke first. "Edith, I have a note for you from Bill."

Edith was staring at her in amazement.

"What's the matter?" Rose asked, puzzled.

"I can't believe you are here," Edith said slowly, drawing Rose into the house.

"Do you mean you wanted me to come to visit you?" Rose asked.

"Why didn't you come?" Edith now asked bluntly.

"Why didn't I come?" Rose echoed in astonishment. "I wanted to come."

"You did? Then why didn't you?"

"Bitter Creek said I couldn't come, that Bill didn't want anyone to come."

"I've been so lonely," Edith said sadly. "I thought nobody cared to visit me."

"We would have come, Kate and the gang," Rose put in eagerly. "All of us wanted to come."

"I didn't know," Edith said mournfully. "I thought nobody liked me."

"I was almost afraid to come today. I thought maybe you wouldn't want to see me."

Edith hugged Rose. "I'm so glad you came. You said you have a note from Bill?"

Rose gave her the note and while Edith read it,

she looked around the room which was very neat and prim.

"He says he loves me," Edith said happily.

"We all know how much he loves you," Rose said. "Bill Doolin has made no secret of how very much he loves you. He calls you his gem."

"I love him so much," Edith whispered. "But, Rose, did you think it would be like this when you fell in love with Bitter Creek?"

"What do you mean?"

"I mean the uncertainty. Never knowing, when you kiss him good-by, if that will be the last time you'll get to kiss him."

Rose nodded. She understood.

"It was so hard for me to get used to the fear that surrounds Bill. Oh, I know he never lets on, but the fear is always with him."

"I know what you mean," Rose put in.

"Bill even sleeps uneasily. He is always instantly alert. It took me quite awhile to get used to his boots standing on the floor, ready and waiting in case he needs them in a hurry."

"I know the whole story well," Rose said sympathetically. "Nearby there's always a belt with a sheathed knife and a holstered, loaded Colt revolver, and a double-barreled shotgun, also loaded, leans against the wall by the bed."

"You do understand," Edith whispered. "You know all about it."

"I know all about it and you and I both know that we love our men above all else and this uncertainty and this fear is part of the price we pay for that love," Rose said definitely.

"I'm so glad you came," Edith said gratefully.

"I've got to get going," Rose said now. "It's a long journey and I've got a big pack of medicine and food to carry."

"How is Bill and how is Bitter Creek?" Edith asked. "I should have asked you that right off, but it was so wonderful just to talk to you."

"Bill is fine and Bitter Creek is improving. He was wounded and is still weak, but he'll be all right as soon as he gets stronger."

"And you're with him taking care of him?" Edith asked.

"Yes, and loving every minute of it," Rose answered.

"I should be with my man, too," Edith said.

"Bill wants you to stay here, doesn't he?"

"I suppose so," Edith countered. "At least that's what he said when he left on that day of the terrible battle."

"I can take a note back to him and you can ask him," Rose suggested.

"No." Edith spoke definitely. "I'm going with you."

"Bill won't like it."

"I can't help what he likes and what he doesn't like," Edith said sharply. "He's kept me here like a doll in a dollhouse."

Rose was silent.

"I wanted to go to the dances at the hotel and be with you and meet the gang, but he wouldn't let me. It was as if he was trying to shield me from life," Edith went on. "One's very soul dries up when one is alone most of the time."

"I told Bitter Creek that you were acting uppity and didn't want to associate with us," Rose said regretfully. "And all the time you wanted to come to the hotel and have a good time with us."

"I used to beg to go but Bill would call me his gem and say that he just wanted to take care of me, to protect me. All I had to look forward to was Bill's returning from one of his mysterious trips."

"I used to wonder what you did all day."

"There were times when I thought I would go mad just waiting for Bill," she cried. "Rose, will you take me with you?"

"I'm afraid of what Bill will say." Rose hesitated.

"If you won't take me with you, I'm going home to my ma and pa," Edith threatened.

"All right, hurry and get ready. It's a long, rough journey, so dress warmly. Do you have a horse?" Rose asked.

"Yes, Bill always kept extra horses. John Kopp takes care of them. He brings my food, too, but he never says two words to me," Edith said.

"I'll go saddle your horse and we'll be off," Rose said, but inwardly, she dreaded their encounter with Bill Doolin.

Chapter 34

When they neared the hideout on the Cimarron, Rose slowed her horse to a walk.

"The guards will stop us," she called to Edith who was following.

"Guards?" Edith asked.

"This place is always under guard," Rose explained. "There're at least ten guards. Here come two of them now."

Sure enough, two men came riding up. "Glad you're back, Cimarron Rose," they greeted her, pulling up beside the two women.

"Who's that with you?"

"This is Bill Doolin's wife, Edith," Rose introduced her. "Edith, this is Montana Bill and Mexican Joe."

Edith acknowledged their greeting while the men stared at her.

Montana Bill, with amazement plainly written on his weather-beaten face, gulped. "You're Bill Doolin's wife? We heard about you, but we ain't never seen you."

Edith smiled. "You'll see me from now on," she said.

"I'm ready," Edith told Rose when they stood at

the heavy door leading into the hideout.

Rose opened the door and immediately there were cries of, "Welcome back, Cimarron Rose." "Glad you made it."

Then there was a heavy silence.

Bill Doolin was at a table playing poker. He had murmured a greeting when Rose entered, but now he looked up.

He dropped his cards and half-rose from his chair.

"Edith," he said.

She went instantly to his side and smiled at him.

He cleared his throat and seemed to have difficulty talking. "What the hell are you doing here?"

His gaze shifted to Rose accusingly.

"Don't blame Rose," Edith said sharply. "I made her bring me along. She didn't want to but I insisted."

"You shouldn't be here," he said woodenly.

"Why shouldn't I be here? I'm your wife. I belong with you," she said definitely.

"It isn't safe," he countered.

"Bill, don't you love me?" she asked now wistfully.

He seemed oblivious of those around him as he took her in his arms and held her close. "I love you more than life itself," he said solemnly. "And because I love you I want you to be safe."

"And because I love *you* I want to be with you," she said very low.

Bitter Creek chimed in jubilantly. "Welcome to our midst, Edith."

Other voices joined in and Edith beamed at the assembled men.

"And to celebrate your coming, I'm going to fix rabbit stew," Tulsa Jack announced.

There was much laughter then.

Later, Rose asked Bitter Creek if he thought Bill would let Edith stay.

"Honey, he'll probably let her stay for a while," Bitter Creek said. "Maybe for as long as you stay."

"That will be forever," she said happily.

"No; while you were gone to Ingalls, Bill told me he has plans made."

"Bill and his plans!" Rose said in disgust. "He's always making plans."

"He has to plan ahead," Bitter Creek said defensively. "The first plan is to get Arizona Tom out of that jail in Stillwater."

"And the second?" she asked dryly.

"He's got a big job planned and—"

She interrupted him. "No, I don't want you to go on any more jobs. It's too dangerous."

"Never tell me what to do," he said harshly.

"It's just because I worry about you when you're on one of Bill Doolin's jobs. I don't want anything to happen to you."

He laughed. "Nothing is going to happen to me."

Later she asked him if he thought Bill and Edith would sleep together in the hideout.

"Of course," he answered readily. "Why wouldn't they sleep together?"

"Do you think they'll . . . ?" She faltered.

He laughed. "What an innocent you are, Rose!

Of course they will. I'll bet they can hardly wait until tonight."

"We don't sleep together." She pouted.

"It's just because I've been so weak," he reminded her. "But I'm getting stronger every day. Another week and I'll be sucking your breasts raw and driving deep into you with love."

She shivered at the thought of anticipated ecstasy and murmured, "Oh, Bitter Creek, I can't wait. I want you in me so bad right now I can't stand it."

"Just be patient. It won't be long," he promised.

As the days went by, Bitter Creek continued to get his strength back. Edith was happy; Red Buck was teaching her to play poker and Montana Bill was teaching her to shoot.

Spring had come. There were buttercups and violets carpeting the ground. Wild lilacs hugged the hideaway door, and everywhere, jays and larks were threading the air with bird song.

Bill Doolin announced one spring morning that the time had come to release Arizona Tom and they would leave that very morning.

"I'd like to go along," Bitter Creek said.

"No, you're not ready," Bill said definitely. "Just be ready when we get ready for the big job in about two weeks. Besides," and he winked at Rose as he spoke, "you had better make hay while the sun shines."

She knew what he meant and she could have hugged him.

When the gang had left, only the guards

stationed outside remained. Edith was practicing shooting and they were finally alone.

The instant the last gang member left, Rose began to peel off her clothes. And Bitter Creek was waiting.

"We've got a lot of time to make up for," she panted, jutting out a bare breast.

He snuggled close to her; then bent down to put her already hardened breast into his mouth. He sucked the nipple gently.

"Harder," she breathed.

He complied, and then ran his teeth over the firm nipple.

"The other one," she cried. "Harder, harder."

He ignored her plea and plunged into her.

As he took her to new heights of ecstasy, she thought that she had never loved him so much.

They clung to each other afterward.

And after a while, he took her again . . . and again.

Chapter 35

Two days later, a triumphant gang returned with Arizona Tom in tow.

They sang; they fired their pistols in celebration, and they had plenty of whiskey.

Bill Doolin explained their victory in rescuing Arizona Tom from the clutches of the law.

"Easiest job we ever pulled," he bragged. "We just marched into old sleepy Stillwater and pulled Arizona Tom out."

"And I was ready to be pulled out," Tom yelled.

"Well, we're all together again and you've got two weeks to rest up for a big job."

"Where we goin'?" Red Buck asked.

Bill Doolin frowned. "You know better than to ask that."

"I was just curious. I know you don't tell nothin' about a job until we get there," Red Buck admitted.

"Then shut up and follow orders," Bill Doolin barked.

For two weeks following Arizona Tom's rescue, the gang rested and played.

There were endless sessions of poker and dancing. Rose and Edith danced as the men sang and took turns dancing with the women.

"Next time I'll bring your violin," Rose promised Bill Doolin.

At the end of the two weeks, Bill assembled the gang together and told them that they would pull out the next day.

"What about us?" Rose asked referring to Edith and herself.

"You two are to go back to Ingalls," Bill Doolin instructed.

Rose thought he was like a general instructing his troops.

"Why can't we stay here and wait for you to return?" Edith asked.

"No," Bill said shortly.

That night, snuggled in Bitter Creek's arms, Rose whispered, "I don't want to go back to Ingalls. I want to stay here."

"Impossible," Bitter Creek answered. "You heard what Bill said."

"Why does he have all the say?" Rose demanded. "Why didn't you speak up?"

"No one questions Bill Doolin," he said firmly and began to nibble on her bare breast. "I'll miss you, my sweetheart."

"And I you. Love me, love me, love me," she whispered fiercely. "Give me something to remember in the weeks ahead."

"I'll send Red Buck in to tell you when we've returned," Bill promised as Rose and Edith departed the next day.

"And we can come back then?" Edith questioned.

"We'll see—"

"I'll bring fixings for a celebration," Rose promised.

"And your fiddle," Edith added.

"We'll see—"

"He wouldn't commit himself," Rose told Edith as they galloped toward Ingalls.

Edith laughed. "We'll just come back. We know where the hideout is."

Rose escorted Edith to the little white house where she unsaddled her horse and exacted a promise from Edith that she would come to visit her at the hotel.

"I want you to meet Kate. Everyone loves Kate," Rose said.

"And her daughter, Amaryllis?" Edith questioned.

Rose laughed. "You're remembering the time she knocked on your door yelling for Bitter Creek?"

"Yes," Edith answered. "She made an awful racket, but Bill sent her on her way quickly enough."

"Yes, you'll meet Amaryllis and at first, you'll think she is very beautiful with her gold hair and her blue eyes, but after a while you won't think she is even pretty. Underneath that white skin she is vicious and mean."

Rose left then to return to the hotel where she was welcomed enthusiastically by Kate. Amaryllis glowered at her and said nothing.

Later Rose asked Kate if Amaryllis was still as unhappy as ever.

"She gets worse every day," Kate replied glumly. "She sits in her room and pouts."

"I thought she would have forgotten all about Matt Hurd by now."

"It's hard for a woman to take rejection," Kate said wisely.

"Do you think he will ever come back to see her?"

Kate shrugged. "It's hard to tell what a man will do. I wish he would come back long enough for her to turn him down."

"She's in love with him," Rose surmised shrewdly. "I don't think she'd ever turn him down. She would fall into his arms."

Several days later, Rose looked up from the registration book to see Bree standing in the doorway.

"Bree!" Rose exclaimed.

The big man stood ill-at-ease, shuffling from one foot to the other.

"I'm surprised to see you. Come in. What brings you to Ingalls?" she asked.

He blurted, "Pa's dyin' and he wants to see you."

"Pa wants to see me?" she echoed astounded.

"He says he wants to talk to you," Bree answered.

"I don't have anything to say to him," Rose replied.

"He is your pa," Bree reminded her.

She looked at him. This didn't sound like the old rough Bree.

"You've changed," she said slowly.

"I've tried to change," he admitted. "I knew all the time that I was getting mean like Pa. Then when Pa got sick and took to his bed, I decided I didn't want to be like Pa."

She stared in amazement.

"The first thing I did was load all of Mary Kahns's furniture on the old buckboard and take

Mary and Ira back to their farm," he explained.

"You got rid of them!" Rose cried. "You got rid of Mary Kahns and Ira?"

"I did. Mary put up an awful fuss. Vowed she wasn't leaving, but I carried her out to the buckboard and threw her in. Ira followed."

Rose went to Bree now and put her arms around him. "Oh, Bree," she whispered. "I'm so glad."

"I've got Genevieve Jenson keeping house for Pa and me. She's Olaf Jenson's widow. He died a few years back and she lost her farm. She was right glad when I asked her to keep house for Pa and me."

"I'll go see Pa," Rose decided suddenly. "One reason I hesitated about going was that I didn't want to see Mary Kahns and Ira."

"Genevieve Jenson is a real lady," Bree said softly.

"I'm anxious to meet her," Rose said.

"Genevieve thought I should bring the buggy," Bree said now.

"You've got a buggy?"

"It's Genevieve's buggy. She brought it with her when she came to the farm," he explained.

"I'll saddle Butter and tie her to the back of the buggy so you won't have to bring me back to Ingalls."

As they drove to the Dunn farm, Rose could not help stealing glances at this brother who was so oddly changed. Even the expression on his face was different.

When they arrived, Genevieve met them at the door and Rose liked her instantly.

She was a rather plain woman with light-brown hair pulled back into a severe knot. Her eyes were hazel, and were offset by thick dark lashes. When she smiled, it transformed her face into a thing of beauty.

They went instantly to Pa's bedside. Rose could hardly believe this shrunken old man was Pa.

"Rose has come to see you," Bree said.

"Rose." Pa's voice quivered as he spoke. "Come close."

She bent her head down to his.

"I'm sorry," he said very low.

She knew instantly what he meant. And it all came back to her now. The memory was so vivid she could smell the hay and the odor of manure as Pa came at her that day, so long ago. She remembered now that she had just finished gathering the eggs and she was all alone. Pa had sneaked up behind her, but she had heard his footsteps and whirled around and looked straight into his beady eyes.

She thought now how his face had been all screwed up ugly-like and he had pushed his whiskers close to her face. He had murmured, "Rose, Rose," and had tried to run his hand up her dress and then he had jerked her still closer and had felt her breasts. At that point, she had told him she would scream and he had seemed to come to his senses.

She shook herself free of the memory as she listened while Pa said again, "I'm sorry."

Bree asked her later what Pa had meant by saying he was sorry.

"Probably," she replied, "he did it because he was so mean to us when we were growing up."

"But he didn't ask to see Ellie and Rebecca," he reasoned.

She shrugged. She would not tell.

Pa died that afternoon. Rose was kneeling by his bedside while he clutched at her hand.

Bree went to get Aunt Celestine and to tell Ellie and Rebecca. He also intended to tell a neighbor, Henry Olmstead, to spread the news of Pa's death and to inform Rev. Timothy Falter.

Genevieve insisted Rose eat something before she started the trek back to Ingalls. She had urged Rose stay the night, as the funeral would be on the morrow, but Rose had declined. She was anxious to get back to Ingalls to see if there was any word from Bitter Creek.

She told Genevieve that she was sure Kate would want to attend the funeral and she would come back early tomorrow.

Before leaving, she hugged Genevieve and told her how glad she was that she had come into Bree's life.

"He's a changed man," Rose said. "He actually seems contented and at peace."

"He was filled with hate," Genevieve said. "And now he has found that life is worth living."

Rose left then, promising to go to Daniel's farm and to tell him and Amanda of Pa's death.

Chapter 36

The next day, Kate insisted Rose use her double-seated buggy so she could ask Edith and Amaryllis to accompany them to Pa's funeral.

Edith accepted the invitation with delight, but Amaryllis curtly refused. "Why the hell do I want to go to an old man's funeral when I didn't even know him?" she asked.

"Out of respect for Rose," Kate answered.

Amaryllis sneered. "I ain't *got* no respect for Rose."

Edith had come into the lobby and was waiting silently.

Amaryllis saw her and whirled at her. "I ain't got no respect for you either. You let a man lock you up and keep you a prisoner."

"Pay no heed to my girl," Kate put in quickly.

The trio left then. It was a singing day, bright with summer sunshine.

At the Dunns', they found the neighbors assembled waiting for the funeral ceremony to begin.

Pa was buried near his two wives and his four children who had been born dead.

The Rev. Timothy Falter was in good form.

As the group walked back to the Dunn farm-house, Bree whispered to Rose, "I'm going to plant some trees and bushes on the graveyard. I remember Daniel wanted to do that years ago and Pa wouldn't let him."

"We're all together here today," Rose said. "You and Daniel and Ellie and Rebecca. We're a family again."

Rebecca and Bill Eckridge and Ellie, Link, Hank, and the baby had arrived shortly before the services so there had been no time for the family to talk.

Now they had a reunion as Ellie proudly displayed her baby girl.

"I named her Rose after you," she told Rose. "I want her to grow up to be like you."

"That's a real compliment if I ever heard one," boomed Kate.

In the middle of their chat, the Rev. Falter raised his arms for silence. "I have an announce-ment to make," he said. "This is a sad occasion as we all know. However, I have been asked to per-form a wedding ceremony this afternoon and it seems a fitting time as so many friends are gathered here to wish this couple well."

Everyone looked surprised. A wedding! Who in this group was about to get married?

Bree and Genevieve Jenson came forward and the ceremony was quickly performed.

"We should have told you," Bree admitted later, "but there wasn't time. I asked Genevieve this morning to marry me and she said, 'Yes.' I thought as long as the preacher was here and the family was here it was a fittin' time."

Rose kissed him and Genevieve and wished them happiness.

"I'm so glad you included me," Edith told Rose as the three of them started back to Ingalls. "It's so nice to be included."

"We love you, Edith," Rose said sincerely. "I guess you are wondering why more tears weren't shed over my pa. He never loved anyone and no one loved him. He was cruel to Bree and Daniel, stropping them sometimes until the blood ran. And he was mean to Ellie and Rebecca and me, too."

"I remember you telling me how much Bree was like your pa," Kate put in now. "He seems so changed."

"He *is* changed," Rose said. "He was so filled with hate for Pa and so afraid the farm wouldn't be his someday. But Genevieve has taught him to love. The hate is all gone now."

In the days following, life went on as usual at the hotel. Rose was busy helping Kate. Amaryllis continued to sulk in her room.

"Doesn't she do anything but weep over Matt Hurd?" Edith asked one afternoon when she had come to visit.

"No," Rose answered. "She decided to help wait on tables, but she was so rude to the customers that Kate fired her."

"I guess she's so unhappy she wants everyone else to be unhappy too," Edith said wisely.

Time passed but there was still no word from the

gang, despite Bill Doolin's promise to send Red Buck into Ingalls. And as the summer was drawing to a close and the leaves were beginning to turn red and gold and the cattails were thick on the lake where Archie Voegele had skated so blithely just before the Battle of Ingalls, Edith came bursting into the lobby of the hotel.

"They're back," Rose cried, seeing her obvious happiness.

"No, no," she exclaimed, her eyes sparkling like stars. "Oh, Rose, I'm so happy. The world is singing. The world is joyous and I'm so happy."

"Tell me," Rose commanded.

"I just stopped at Dr. Dragg's and he confirmed it. I'm going to have a baby."

"I'm happy for you," Rose said slowly. "Do you think Bill will be happy?" She could not help but ask the question.

"I don't know. I don't want to think about that. I don't want anything to keep me from being happy today," she went on joyously.

Rose sighed. She could not imagine that Bill Doolin would be very happy at the prospect of his being a father.

And then on an early fall day, a visitor came to the hotel — a squarely built man who came into the lobby slowly, big hat in hand.

Kate, at the registration desk, looked up in surprise.

"Matt Hurd!"

"Howdy, Miss Kate," the man greeted her politely.

"What the hell are you doing here?" she asked.

And then, not waiting for him to answer, she glanced at the star shining on his coat. "I see," she went on sarcastically, "that you have a real star."

"I'm sorry it all turned out the way it did," he said humbly.

"Sorry?" the woman rasped. "Sorry? You broke my daughter's heart and you come back here to say you're sorry!"

"Could I see Amaryllis?"

"What do you want to do?" she taunted. "Hurt her some more?"

"If I could just talk to her," he begged.

"I'll see if she wants to talk to you," Kate answered, but she knew the answer before she started up the stairs.

She knocked gently on the door to Amaryllis' room.

"What do you want?" Amaryllis asked sharply.

"There's someone downstairs who wants to talk to you," the mother said.

"Who is it?"

"Come on down and see who it is," Kate requested softly.

Amaryllis spoke angrily. "I don't want to see anyone."

"I'll tell him to go away," Kate said and turned to go back downstairs. "I'll tell Matt Hurd you don't want to see him."

Instantly, Amaryllis was at the door. "Mamma, did you say Matt was here?"

"Yes, but I'll tell him you don't care to see him."

"Don't you dare. Tell him to wait. Tell him I'll

be downstairs in a minute."

Kate went downstairs and told Matt Hurd that Amaryllis would be down shortly.

Presently, Amaryllis came dancing down the stairs. Her cheeks were rose-tinted with excitement and her eyes sparkled.

"Matt," she said simply and her voice was choked.

"Amaryllis," he said very low and rushed to the foot of the stairs to greet her.

They went then into the sitting room where he had told her good-by months ago.

Chapter 37

Hours passed before Amaryllis and Matt emerged.

Amaryllis was happier than she had been for many months.

Kate was waiting.

"Mamma, Matt and I are going to be married," she cried joyously.

Kate did not smile as she asked simply, "When?"

"As soon as he catches the Doolin gang," Amaryllis sang out.

Rose, coming down the stairs, heard her words and paused.

"He's going to catch the gang and then we're going to get married and Matt is going to resign his job and we'll settle down on a cattle farm," Amaryllis said breathlessly.

"Really," Kate's voice was cold and unbelieving.

"Yes, Mamma," Amaryllis cried turning to Matt. "Tell Mamma. Tell her that that's what is going to happen."

He looked embarrassed and said nothing.

Amaryllis had flung herself at him and rested her cheek against his shoulder.

"It is true," he admitted. "I didn't intend for

Amaryllis to reveal all our plans, but she has, and it's all right."

"Do you think you'll actually catch the Doolin gang?" Kate asked.

"It's just a matter of time," he said firmly.

Matt saw Rose standing transfixed on the stairs and asked politely, "And how is your family, Rose?"

"My pa died. Bree got rid of Mary Kahns and Ira and he's married to a very nice woman named Genevieve," Rose answered.

"It's good to see you again," he said.

"I'll always be grateful to you," Rose went on, "for putting Pa back in his farm. But I have to say this, Matt Hurd, you will *never* capture the Doolin gang."

"That remains to be seen," he said softly. "I must be going now."

He took Amaryllis in his arms, their lips met, his hands locked tightly about her shoulders, and her own hands were crushed against his heart.

"Until we meet again," he said very low.

"I'll be waiting," she promised, as she walked to the door with him.

He turned back to nod good-by to Rose and Kate and then was gone.

Amaryllis was radiant as she said, "He did come back."

"What did he say about your rushing out of the hotel to warn him of the ambush?" Kate asked.

"He thought I was mighty brave," Amaryllis said, smiling.

"You were almost killed for being so brave," her

mother said dryly.

"He said his first impulse was to jump from his horse and drag me to safety," Amaryllis went on.

"But he didn't," Kate cried triumphantly. "He didn't. Poor old Dr. Dragg was the brave one."

"I know, Mamma, but you have to remember that Matt is a lawman," Amaryllis reminded her.

"I just want you to be happy," Kate said quietly. "But I must admit I agree with Rose. The Doolin gang will never be captured."

"I wouldn't bet on that," Amaryllis said flippantly and was singing as she left the room.

"She believes every word he says," Kate mourned.

"She's in love with him," Rose pointed out.

"Her happiness will mean your unhappiness," Kate observed.

"If Matt and his lawmen haven't caught the Doolin gang by now, I don't think they ever will," Rose said slowly.

"He did seem sincere when he said that Amaryllis was telling the truth about his retiring and getting a cattle farm," Kate said.

"Oh, yes, I don't doubt that he is sincere," Rose agreed. "He's getting older and no doubt, would like to settle down."

"Well, he'd make my little girl mighty happy if he kept that promise."

"Amaryllis was a changed person after his visit. She truly loves him," Rose said.

"And now she will live on hope," Kate said bitterly. "Just as I lived on hope so many years ago. I kept hoping that Spider would come back. But as the days became weeks and the weeks months I knew he had no intention of coming back to marry me. It's a terrible thing to give up hope."

Later Rose was thinking of Kate's words about giving up hope and had just about decided that her hope of Bitter Creek returning was fading when Red Buck bounced merrily into the hotel one night.

He demanded whiskey and, after being served, told Rose that the gang had returned to the hideout on the Cimarron and that Bitter Creek wanted her to join him.

"And Edith?" she asked. "Does Bill Doolin want Edith to come."

"He does and he doesn't," Red Buck admitted, gulping down his whiskey and raising his cup for more.

"What do you mean by that, 'He does and he doesn't'?"

"He wants her with him and yet he wants to protect her," the man explained.

"Well, he can't have it both ways," Rose said sharply.

"I know, I know," he said soothingly.

"Do we tell Edith or not that we are going to the Cimarron?" she asked.

"Yes. Let her make up her own mind if she wants to go," he decided.

"She'll want to go."

"Do you want me to go tell her?"

"No, I'll go. You enjoy your whiskey. I think it best if we leave at dawn. You can stay the night at the hotel," she advised.

"In that case," he roared happily, "I'll have more."

At the little white house, she told Edith of their plan to leave at dawn for the hideout on the Cimarron.

"I wonder if Bill really wants me to come," she pondered.

"He loves you," Rose reminded her.

"Yes, I know."

"Are you going to tell him about the baby?" Rose asked.

"No, not yet."

"But why not?" Rose asked, surprised. "Why don't you tell him?"

"He might not be pleased," Edith said slowly. "I love him so much that I want only to please him."

"Red Buck and I leave at dawn."

"I'll be ready," Edith promised.

Chapter 38

The gang was in a jubilant mood. Their trip had been a huge success. They had made seven raids on banks and had garnered much loot.

They greeted Rose and Edith with open arms.

Immediately on seeing Bitter Creek, Rose was whirled away into that enchanted world where he and she alone dwelled. Just the grip of his big hand on hers, just the sound of his voice, just the meeting of their eyes were enough to instill in her a happiness that was almost unbearable in its intensity.

Bill Doolin seemed delighted to see Edith. Rose watched him as he greeted his wife and she wished that Edith would tell him her news of the coming baby. She was curious to know his reaction.

The weeks went by and life was a happy dream for Rose.

Then one morning, Bill Doolin told Bitter Creek, Rose, and Edith he had a surprise for them.

"There's a bank in Southwest City, Missouri, that is ready and waiting to be picked. It'll be an easy job and we'll go and pluck it," he said.

"Us?" Rose blurted. "You mean Edith and me?"

"Sure," he said easily. "You'll enjoy it and you

can see firsthand how your men do a job."

Edith had turned white and Rose knew she was thinking of her condition. But she didn't bat an eyelash. She smiled happily at her husband and said she was ready.

"We'll take Red Buck and Montana Bill," Bill Doolin planned aloud.

"I'm afraid," Edith confided to Rose later that day.

"Why don't you tell Bill about the baby? Then he won't want you to go on the bank robbery."

"I can't hide behind the baby," Edith said softly. "Bill would think I'm a coward."

They left early the next morning. The sky was barred with red and gold as they rode away from the hideout.

It was a long, hard ride and when night came and they had bedded down, Rose breathed a sigh of relief. She was tired. Edith looked white and exhausted.

Bill Doolin had coffee boiling at dawn. He was on fire with the plan which he now explained in detail.

He would ride into Southwest City and survey the surroundings. Edith and Rose would wait outside the town for their return.

Rose was thankful for this information. She had envisioned her and Edith entering the bank with drawn guns.

At noon, Bill Doolin, Bitter Creek, Red Buck, and Montana Bill entered the town.

The robbery was an easy one. The two bank

tellers handed over the money. They were petrified with fright.

However, as the outlaws swung up on their horses, a lawman ran out into the street from the jail.

Montana Bill took aim and killed him instantly.

A window was thrown up across the street and a shotgun roared. A burst of buckshot hit Bill Doolin in the forehead.

Almost blinded by the blood, but still firing, Doolin led them out of town.

A posse followed in close pursuit, but the gang's horses were always of the best, and they soon outdistanced the posse.

But when they had circled back to meet Rose and Edith, and rode up to them, Edith took one look at Bill with blood streaming down his face, and she fainted.

Bitter Creek hoisted her in front of him. Montana Bill grabbed the bridle of Edith's horse and they were off.

That night when they bedded down, Edith cried, the tears streaming down her face.

"I'm sorry I fainted," she wept. "You'll think I'm a coward."

"Of course not," Bill Doolin assured her. "It must have been a real shock to see me with my head all bloody."

"I thought you were going to die."

"The buckshot just grazed my head," he went on. "But I must have been a gruesome sight."

Rose, listening, was waiting for Edith to tell him that she was in the family way. But Edith said nothing more.

"Tell him. Tell him," Rose silently urged. "Now, when he is so loving, is the time to tell him."

The next morning they proceeded back to the Cimarron hideout.

Rose was glad to be back. The trip had tired her.

She was lying in her bunk one afternoon trying to nap when she heard Edith and Bill Doolin talking.

The gang, except the guards, had gone to do a bank robbery job at a nearby town.

She heard Bill say, "Edith, I think you would be better off in Ingalls."

"Why do you say that?" she queried.

"You seem so pale lately."

"And I'm tired, too, but then Rose said the trip to Southwest City tired her, too. We're not used to such a long trip and there was the fear we felt while we were waiting wondering if you and Bitter Creek would be killed."

The man laughed. "No danger of our being killed. We lead charmed lives."

She did not laugh.

"You've got to toughen up, my beautiful angel. As Bill Doolin's wife you've got to be tough."

"I want to be your wife and not your widow," she said wistfully.

He sighed and said nothing.

"Bill," she said softly. "Bill, we are going to have a baby."

There was complete silence following this announcement.

Rose waited with bated breath.

"We are what?"

"I said we are going to have a baby," she repeated.

"We can't," he said definitely. "We can't have a baby. I have enough to do now worrying about you and your safety. We cannot have a baby."

"What do you propose I do? Take doses of tansy root?" she asked sarcastically.

"Yes, tansy root or whatever it takes to get rid of it," he instructed harshly.

"I will not," she cried stubbornly. "I intend to have our baby. If you don't want it, I will go back to Lawton to Ma and Pa."

"Edith, dearest, please understand," he begged. "A baby would be like a millstone around our necks."

"If you loved me, you would want our baby," she mourned.

"Loving you has nothing to do with it."

"I'll go back to Ingalls tomorrow and then onto Lawton," she planned.

"Maybe . . . maybe now would be the time to hang up the guns," he faltered as he voiced the words.

"Oh, Bill, my darling, if only you would," she cried.

"Would you like that?"

"I would be so happy. We could live like other people. We could have our baby and a farm and live in quiet and peace. I could plant violets by the door and we could have trees," she said happily.

"Let me think about it," he said.

Rose could hardly believe her ears. She had actually heard Bill Doolin talk about hanging up his guns! Immediately her thoughts soared. Bitter Creek could hang up his guns, too, and she, too, could plant flowers and have a kitchen with cups and saucers and plates.

She told Bitter Creek that evening what she had overheard. First she had insisted that they walk down toward the lake and there, in utter privacy, she told him everything.

Bitter Creek laughed and said that she had imagined Bill Doolin's talk about hanging up his guns. Right now he had about fifteen jobs planned.

"I heard him," Rose insisted.

"You dreamed it," he jeered.

She was silent for a while, but she was seething inwardly. When she spoke, it was to ask mildly, "If Bill did hang up his guns . . . No, don't interrupt me. . . . Just suppose he did. . . . Would you lead the gang?"

"That's one decision I won't have to make," Bitter Creek said definitely. "Bill Doolin will never quit the outlaw trail."

A week later, Doolin asked Rose if she would escort Edith back to Ingalls.

Rose, reluctantly, agreed. She not only didn't want to leave Bitter Creek. She wanted to hang around to see what Bill Doolin was going to do.

Chapter 39

After delivering Edith to the little white house and exacting a promise from her to take care of herself and check with Dr. Dragg if she didn't feel well, Rose went to the hotel.

Kate was glad to see her.

"This town just ain't the same without the Doolin gang. It's just too quiet," Kate observed.

"Yes, I wish things were like they used to be. We had such exciting times at the dances."

"It's just too quiet now," Kate mourned.

"How's Amaryllis?" Rose asked.

"Happy as a lark," Kate answered. "Matt writes to her and she moons over the letters and spends half her time writing back to him."

"I guess he does love her."

"I don't know," Kate said doubtfully. "In his way, I suppose he does. But I think if he truly loved her, he would forget his aim to capture the Doolin gang."

"It's his dream, I guess," Rose said. "It would really be a feather in his hat if he could capture the gang before he quits being a lawman."

"You're right and we all have a dream," Kate answered seriously.

"What's your dream, Kate?" Rose asked curiously. "What would you rather have than anything else in the world?"

"I would want Amaryllis to be happy, but not if it made you unhappy. And what is your dream?" she asked.

"To be with Bitter Creek always," Rose answered. "I want us to have a house of our own where I can cook for him and take care of him. I want us to go away and start a new life where no one knows Bitter Creek. I want us to go someplace where he will be safe, where he won't have to be afraid someone will shoot him in the back."

"Have you changed your mind about getting married?" Kate asked.

"Yes. I want to marry him in front of a preacher. I know we made vows to each other when we were alone in the woods and I felt married, but I want to stand before a preacher and say, 'I do.' "

Rose stayed the night at the hotel and left at dawn for the hideout on the Cimarron.

She found the gang getting their guns in top shape.

"Are you going out on a job?" she asked Bitter Creek.

"Jobs," he answered briefly.

Later, when they were alone, he said, "I know I laughed at you when you spoke of Bill Doolin quitting, but now I wonder."

"Why?" she asked.

"He's called all the gang in. Some of them have been holed up deep in the Creek Nation at the Outlaw's Cave. I told you he had many jobs planned. He is like a wild man planning each one. In fact, he is dividing the gang up to get the jobs done in a hurry."

"Do you think he is getting ready to hang up his guns?" she asked and her voice trembled with eagerness to know.

"I don't know, but it seems to me he is trying to get together a nest egg."

"Oh, Bitter Creek, isn't that wonderful?" she breathed.

He shrugged, but did not answer.

The next day the men who had been at the Outlaw's Cave rode in, about twelve of them—each one anxious to tell Bill Doolin what had happened.

Bill designated Tulsa Jack to tell the story.

Tulsa Jack plunged into his tale with gusto. "We heard the signal from the guards and we were ready. Here comes that lawman, Matt Hurd, real bold-like."

Matt Hurd! Rose heard the name and was startled. He really was making every effort to find the gang. But walking into their hideout was the same as committing suicide!

"He came in and said he had lost his way. He didn't know there where ten Colts aimed at his head! I told him to go back the same way he came and out he went."

"Why didn't you kill him?" Red Buck asked.

"Some of the men were mad because I didn't give the signal to shoot him, but I think Matt Hurd is too good a man to get shot in the back," Tulsa Jack explained.

"Right you are," Bill Doolin agreed heartily. "The Doolin gang does not shoot anyone in the back."

"I knew Matt Hurd would be back with all his lawmen so as we was aimin' to come right away, we headed out as soon as he was out of sight."

"Good work," Bill Doolin complimented.

He then went into great detail to outline each job. Each group would have four jobs. Tulsa Jack, Red Buck, and Montana Bill would be in charge of the various groups. Bill Doolin would have his own group.

"You can ride with Bitter Creek," he told Rose. "That way the Newcombs will have a double share of the loot."

She thought this was a strange thing for him to say and asked Bitter Creek about it later.

"It does seem odd," Bitter Creek agreed. "But Bill is doing so many odd things lately, we'll just have to go along."

There were fifteen, including Rose, under Bill Doolin's command. Rose surmised, and rightly, that Doolin had selected the jobs with the biggest loot. She waited at the outskirts of the towns where the banks were to be robbed. Then as the gang streamed past afterward, she would join them at breakneck speed.

The fifteen jobs were finished, each triumphantly.

Bill Doolin was jubilant. "And now," he cried happily, "we will have a celebration. We will have a real celebration of our success in fifteen robberies."

Rose told Bitter Creek that Bill Doolin seemed unusually happy.

Bitter Creek was puzzled. He couldn't quite put his finger on it, but he knew Bill Doolin well enough from their many years of friendship to know that Bill always had a reason for everything.

"Cimarron Rose," Bill Doolin said, "I want you to go into Ingalls and get Edith. The celebration won't be perfect without her."

Before leaving, Rose asked Bitter Creek if he thought Bill Doolin was going to hang up his guns. Did he suppose that was the reason for the celebration?

"No, I think he's glad that all the jobs turned out so well."

"What will you do if he does hang up his guns for good?" she asked.

"What do you mean?" he asked.

"Well, you're first lieutenant. If he quits, would you lead the gang?" she asked bluntly.

Bitter Creek looked at her for a long moment and said nothing.

"It would be the Newcomb gang," Rose said simply, her green eyes wide.

Bitter Creek laughed. "That sounds great. I like that. The Newcomb gang!"

Rose sighed. "It's a big responsibility to tell forty or fifty men what to do."

"I can handle it. I'd make a damned good leader," he cried.

"Oh, I know that, my darling," she assured him. "I'm not questioning your ability to lead the gang."

"What is it then?" he demanded. "You try to tell me what to do, but you won't marry me. I don't need someone to question my ability to lead the gang. I need someone to trust me."

"I trust you," she cried, somehow affronted. "I've shown you how much I love you. I've ridden with you and shared danger with you. I couldn't do more even if I were your wife."

He was not listening. He had turned away.

But just before she set out for the long journey to Ingalls, he came to her and put his arms around her and whispered, "Forgive me. I love you."

She looked at him, her face radiant. Her green eyes glowed like amethysts.

"Whatever you do is fine with me," she said very low. "Wherever you go, I want to be right beside you."

In Ingalls, she went to see Kate, who was, as usual, delighted to see her.

She would have loved to tell Kate about her suspicions that Bill Doolin was about to hang up his guns, but she dared not!

Amaryllis came sauntering into the lobby while Rose and Kate were talking.

"So your back?" she asked, smiling.

Rose was surprised at her cordial tone.

"I'm not mad at you anymore," Amaryllis said. "I don't give a damn about the Doolin gang and neither does Matt. He's promised he's going to forget all about the gang and he's going to quit being a lawman and we're going to get married."

"I'm glad to hear that," Rose said heartily. "I really am, Amaryllis. I truly would like to know that you are happy."

Amaryllis' blue eyes were stars. "As Mrs. Matt Hurd, I will be the happiest woman on earth."

Later, at the little white house, she told Edith the news imparted to her by the radiant Amaryllis.

"So he's given up hope of capturing the Doolin gang," Edith said slowly. "If he only knew!"

"Knew what?"

Edith evaded the question neatly. "Bill sent for me? What else did he say?"

"That you are to come and help celebrate."

Rose had hardly spoken the words when Edith grabbed her in a bear hug.

Tears were running down her cheeks as she cried, "Oh, Rose, it means that Bill is quitting the outlaw trail. It means that we can start a new life."

Rose kissed her, but her heart was leaden.

Did this mean that Bitter Creek would become the new leader? Did it mean that her home would be forever the hideout on the Cimarron? Did it mean that she would never have her own little kitchen where she could hang green-and-white polka-dotted curtains at the windows? And did this mean she would never have dainty teacups, but would have to use the heavy mugs used by the gang?

Edith was talking happily. "I've packed as much as I can carry on an extra horse. And I've got Bill's fiddle."

"Yes, don't forget the fiddle. We can't have a real celebration without it."

"Oh, Rose, I've been so happy, rambling on about starting a new life, that I didn't stop to think what this will mean to you," Edith said remorsefully.

Rose sighed.

"Do you think Bitter Creek will take over the leadership of the gang?" Edith asked.

"I don't know," Rose answered truthfully. "I don't think Bitter Creek actually believed that Bill would ever not lead the gang."

"I can hardly believe it even now," Edith admitted. "But when you said that Bill asked me to come and we would have a big celebration, that was what we had decided would mean that he was giving up the outlaw trail."

"Where will you go?"

"I don't know, but I'm sure Bill has a plan. He always has a plan," she said, smiling tenderly to herself.

Rose now suggested that they rest for a few hours and start out.

When they left the little white house, Edith turned back to look at it in the moonlight. "My little white house," she whispered. "My little honeymoon cottage. Good-by."

They stopped only to rest the horses and nibble at the biscuits and salt port Edith had prepared so they were both weary when they neared the turnoff to the hideout.

"We're almost there," Edith said, breathing a sigh of relief. "Won't it be wonderful to see Bill and Bitter Creek?"

Rose nodded. She was watching an approaching figure on a horse. There was something vaguely familiar about him, she thought, as he neared.

He wore a wide black hat and a black frock coat. She had seen that hat and coat before! But where? And then it came to her. This man was the Rev. Enos Perry, the preacher who had married her brother, Daniel, and Amanda.

She could hardly believe her eyes!

"Aren't you Rev. Perry?" she called as he pulled abreast.

"Yes," he answered and then he recognized her and he was all smiles.

"Edith," Rose said, "you know the way from here. Hurry and tell Bitter Creek to come and meet me here with two witnesses. Today is his wedding day!"

Edith stared her amazement, then hurried off at a fast trot.

The entranceway to the road that led to the hideaway was cleverly camouflaged with thick brush and trees, but Rose knew Edith could find it.

While they waited, she explained the situation to the preacher. He said he would be delighted to perform a marriage ceremony so Rose jumped from her horse and began to gather a bouquet of goldenrod and Queen Anne's lace.

The exquisite fall day was sweet with the fragrance of flowers. Bird song filled the air and soft white clouds floated in an azure sky.

Happiness was humming in her veins and singing in her ears as she waited, chatting with the minister.

At the same time, Rose and the reverend heard the horses' hoofs.

She waited breathlessly as Bitter Creek, Red Buck, and Tulsa Jack came clattering up.

Then Bitter Creek's arms were around her and their eyes were close together as he whispered, "You've decided, my darling?"

"Yes, yes," she cried. "Do you still want to marry me?"

"I love you," he said for answer.

The ceremony was a short one so presently the preacher, endowed generously by an exuberant Bitter Creek, went on his way. Rose, Bitter Creek, Red Buck, and Tulsa Jack headed for the hideout.

There they were greeted with open arms by the gang and Bill Doolin announced that the celebration would begin. Not only were they celebrating the fifteen successful robberies, but also the wedding of the Newcombs.

And celebrate they did!

Whiskey flowed like water and Bill Doolin played his violin hour after hour.

The hideout rang with laughter and happiness for two long days and nights.

Then Doolin called a time of rest.

"Now what?" Rose asked.

"That, Mrs. Newcomb," he said, smiling. "we will have to see."

They did not have long to wait. Soon Bill Doolin called everyone together.

Lamps were lighted in a far corner of the room and with the sun filtering in there was a homey atmosphere in the hideout. But when Bill raised his hands for silence, a hush fell over the room.

"We've had a great time celebrating," he began, and then stopped.

Rose noticed how husky his voice was. She glanced at Edith and saw that she was staring at her husband and her lovely face was radiant.

He began again. "We've had a great time together. We've stood by each other and we've trusted each other. Now the time has come to part." He paused to clear his throat.

"Part?" The word echoed in the air as his astonished listeners repeated it.

"I'm hanging up my guns," he said definitely. "The Doolin gang will be no more."

There were cries of protest. He raised his hands

for silence again.

"I'm asking Bitter Creek Newcomb to be your leader," he went on, and there was applause in the room.

Rose waited with bated breath. She thought silently, Don't accept the offer, my darling. *Please* don't accept.

Bitter Creek went forward now and stood next to Bill Doolin.

"I thank you, Bill," he said slowly, sincerely. "But I, too, am now a married man and the time has come for me to hang up my guns."

Rose rushed forward to his side. His arms were around her and she raised her eyes to his; all her beauty and sweetness were his for one dizzying moment in a long kiss.

There was much applause now as Rose and Bitter Creek, hand in hand, left the front of the long room.

"And what will happen to the gang?" she asked as she gathered their few belongings together.

"Oh, they'll probably select Tulsa Jack for their leader. They'll drift along for a while and then they'll split up," he predicted easily.

"I'm ready," she announced. "Are we going with Edith and Bill? I suppose Bill has a plan."

Bitter Creek laughed. "Bill always has a plan. We'll go with them to Texas and then we'll probably go farther."

She smiled at him. Her green eyes were wells of happiness.

"Is that all right with you, my darling?" he asked tenderly.

Her beautiful face was radiant with hidden glory as she whispered, "I will follow you to the ends of the earth and beyond."